TAINTED BEAUTY

by

A. C. DYKE

ISBN-13: 978-1518687693
ISBN-10: 1518687695

DEDICATION

To my wife for her patience and understanding.

CONTENTS

ACKNOWLEDGMENTS

Regarding the Castlemorton Invasion (Chapter 2), this was researched by the author after the event, via a West Mercia Police report, interview with the police and Parish Council, local media (Malvern Gazette), and TV reports.

Unfortunately, like so many incidents of this kind, it was difficult to obtain the views of the participants.

The characters involved in this story are fictional.

My thanks to all those who participated.

*

Although not prevalent at Castlemorton at the time, there is however, a good example of the authoritarian attitude of the 1980s in what was a Channel 4 documentary, entitled "Operation Solstice – The Battle of the Beanfield". Available on DVD from the Culture Shop, Bristol.

www.cultureshop.org.

Tainted ideological policies and decisions made in the past by the dominant ruling culture, can lead to negative consequences for settled, cohesive communities, tainting the beauty, leading to, in certain cases, counter-cultural responses.

PROLOGUE

This is a modern story about obsessive love and revenge set against a background of the destructive nature of a rapidly changing society. However it is perhaps most importantly a reflective criticism of modern times, particularly with reference to rural cities and towns, whereby drugs and associated crime, the disease of the big city, has spread to the countryside; tainting the beauty. It also reflects upon the tainting nature of politics and decisions made which affect the future of societies to come and the creation of sub-cultures, regarded as deviant or otherwise.

Nathan, the lead character, has an obsessional love attachment to Rosalind, a woman one or two years older than himself. They meet during the illegal rave, New Age Traveller, festival period of the early 1990s. During the Castlemorton invasion, Rosalind, a serious drug addict, starts receiving supplies of heavy drugs from the notorious Grivens brothers. Towards the end of the rave, Nathan finds Rosalind in such a serious condition that he believes she is dead. As a result he attacks Darren Grivens, killing him.

Released from prison twenty-three years later, Nathan returns in the hope of meeting up and renewing his relationship with Rosalind, who he had later learnt that she had survived. Thoughts of her had kept him alive mentally whilst in prison and as a consequence had become obsessional. However, unknown to him, Rosalind had ended up with an acquired brain injury. Not only that but she'd married the young police officer who had been allocated the role to watch over her whilst she is in a coma at the hospital.

The other main problem for Nathan returning to his home town was that the other Grivens brother, Dwayne, was now a big-time drug dealer/major criminal in the area. Aware of Nathan's release and having vowed to get vengeance for the killing of his brother, Grivens now had the opportunity to gain revenge.

The ultimate result is that it leads to a bloody conclusion.

This book has an emotive message about the danger of drugs on society, particularly even now in rural areas. This is set against the background of the current financial and political decline in society and the tainted beauty of communities.

The story starts in the early 1990s and then moves to the present time. The 1980s/90s was a period during the Thatcher years, where there was the destruction of traditional industries, with the knock-on effect on communities, leading to a great deal of despair about work and the future in general. Many young and perhaps not so young people, not accepting the harsh political culture of the time, of recession and long-term unemployment, dropped-out and took to the road, with old buses, VW vans and other means of transport which provided many with a place to live. For a while the country was beset by groups know as New-Age Travellers, a drop-out, revolutionary sub-culture, with links to the protest movement, traveling from festival to festival and drugs became an element of that danger and exclusion from mainstream society. Other than the annual Summer Solstice at Stonehenge which created many problems in the area, these activities led to two major events: the "Battle of the Beanfield", where police herded travellers onto a field of beans, attacking them and their vehicles, but the culmination of these activities led to the invasion of Castlemorton Common in Worcestershire. This event made national newspapers and TV headlines for a number of days. Although this story starts with this event, the rest of the story is fictional. As far as it is aware no one was killed at Castlemorton, even though there may have been some who felt like it.

During this period of history there was a great deal of political and industrial unrest, leading to events like "The Battle of Orgreave" (miner's dispute), "Fortress Wapping" (printer's dispute) and the "Poll Tax Riots". As well as "The Battle of the Beanfield" these events all involving a heavy police presence.

Novels, films etc., particularly in the crime genre, tend to present the problem of drugs as a big city problem. Drug crime just takes place in cities such as London, Manchester or Birmingham and remains rather anonymous to everyone other than those involved. But the truth is that it affects all aspects of society. So it is not by chance that the story is set in a more rural area. It was felt necessary to show that it exists everywhere and isn't just an aspect of life that "doesn't exist around here – it just happens in the big cities". It was felt that this may have a greater impact, plus the fact it is a major problem now.

The author set the story around the City of Worcester, not just because of his personal knowledge of the area, but because it was the logical location being so close to Castlemorton. Also like every other town and city in this country it has its own fair share of drug related problems.

The question this novel asks is does society ever change for the better, or is it the age-old story that the powerful gain more power at the expense of the poor.

The book has a number of related themes: the tainted beauty of communities through political and social change, the ensuing tainted beauty of society by drug abuse and the tainted beauty of life due to changes that only benefit a few to the detriment of the many.

CHAPTER 1

THE RETURN

'Twenty-three years for killing scum. Twenty-three fucking years!' brooded Nathan Hancock, staring out of the grubby windows of the train as it sped past the green fields of Worcestershire. In the distance he could see the outline of the Malvern Hills as the train reached the outskirts of Worcester.

He thought about the area he was returning to and wondered how much it had changed. He'd heard that some guy on the TV had made out that this area and the surrounding rural towns were experiencing the problem of drugs; he didn't know much about it at this stage. He'd witnessed the drug culture of the 80s and early 90s, which he knew had its problems but then it was generally confined to a certain community, such as the New Agers he'd lived with before he was arrested. But the tainting of an area he knew so well saddened him. Inside prison he had seen the pushers and users of drugs and it was something he felt was downgrading society. He felt it was now no longer just the case of referring to drugs purely as an inner city problem, where the problem became hidden or even accepted, the problem was being more open; tainting the beauty of rural life.

From Nathan's experience, Worcester on the

surface always gave the impression of being a middle-class cathedral city, but with a low-income economy and a reduction in the need for traditional skilled labour over the years, deprivation lay smouldering under the surface. Nathan could well guess that the breakdown of community led to the vulnerable taking solace from the friendly, or not so friendly, drug pusher who called.

Nathan wondered if he was crazy returning; he knew there would be a reception for him, waiting to settle old scores. But he was on parole and the prison welfare had arranged for him to stay at a parole hostel. After all he had nowhere else to go; his father had died of a stroke a few years previous, his mother had disappeared down to the South Coast with some fellow, and his elder brother had emigrated to Canada ten years before. However his main need to return was based on his desire to check out the relationship that had obsessively gnawed at his mind all the time he'd spent in prison. A relationship, or at least the thoughts of it, that had kept him together body and soul over the last twenty-three years.

The train headed for its first stop in Worcester at Shrub Hill Station. Nathan smiled to himself as he remembered the last time he was at this station. It was twenty-five years previous when he stood waiting for a train to take him for an interview at Birmingham University; his days as a student lay before him. He remembered the incident clearly. Whilst stood on the platform it was announced over the station speaker, in a rather jubilant voice, that Margaret Thatcher had stood down as Prime Minister. The few people on the platform showed their joy by jumping up and down with their arms in the air. Quite a surprising sight, thought Nathan, for what had always been considered a rather reserved city.

The train rolled into Shrub Hill Station. *No change here*, he thought, staring at the dreary platform. His feelings twenty-odd years previous were that London and the surrounding Home Counties didn't give a shit about places in the West Midlands like Worcester, the North Midlands, and even less about the north of the country. They were like a country within a country. His feelings on seeing the station now had not changed his views.

He knew he should be getting off because the hostel was in that area of the city. But he needed to get to the Westside to renew old acquaintances. However, as soon as the train arrived at the station he knew that even if he wanted to he couldn't have got off there. Lurking in the station entrance, out of general sight, scouring the scene stood Grivens. Dwayne Grivens was the older brother of the scum that he had killed. Although he hadn't seen him all those years and even though he looked a couple of stone heavier, one never forgot his cruel but imposing, towering appearance. His shaven head made him look even more menacing, but even with that he was easily recognisable.

Moving openly on the station platform were four of his hired thugs, most of whom appeared to be young thin-faced junkies. Clocking every passenger that alighted from the train, they clearly knew who they were looking for. The prison grapevine had clearly kept Grivens informed of his release and current appearance.

The train doors closed and as the train moved forward Grivens suddenly caught sight of Nathan. Grivens gave him an evil smirk, patted the side of his waist and then chillingly drew the flat of his hand across his throat in a cutting motion. The motion across the throat was obvious to Nathan and what he had heard in prison informed him of the reasons for the pat on his side; Grivens carried a 1kg club hammer attached to his belt. This he used to keep all opposition in line and because of this he had gained the nickname of 'Sledgehammer'. Any drug dealer who came onto his patch was dealt with a crippling blow to their left hand. Grivens found this a more effective treatment than just killing the opposition; it spread his reputation much more effectively and kept the police off his back. If anyone dared to continue their activities, even with a crushed left hand, then the ultimate punishment was the crushing of the right hand as well. Some of the gun-toting interlopers from Birmingham soon found that they could no longer handle a gun.

Although Grivens' father was a violent alcoholic who had died from the drink, his mother was a religious prude. It was thought that he'd got his ideas for his punishments from his bible-quoting mother. Misquoting the bible for his own purposes, he would state to his victims: 'If your left hand offend me then it will be dealt with and if your right hand should further offend me then that will be dealt with too.'

The train left Shrub Hill Station and moved on towards Foregate Street, the central station. Nathan needed to get off there to make his way to the Westside. There was no reception party at the station as he got off. Before setting off for the Westside he decided to drop into the little station café, which was situated in the corner of the platform. He needed a coffee, but also he was curious to know if a woman by the name of Jacqui still worked there. Jacqui was a warm, friendly young woman whose image had stayed in his mind during prison. Many a time he had spent in the café as a young man, flirting, chatting and laughing with Jacqui. One of the many images that had kept a young man's body and mind together during black periods in prison. However she was no longer there. Disappointed, he ordered a coffee and a packet of sandwiches. Drinking the coffee in a few minutes, he picked up the sandwiches, walked out of the café and towards the station entrance.

To his horror, emerging out of the entrance onto the platform were the same thugs he had seen at the previous station. Coming face to face, both parties froze for a few seconds. The thugs were already showing signs of breathlessness after climbing the forty-nine steps from the street up to the platform. Because of this, Nathan was the first to respond. Quickly looking around, he realised he had no place to run; the station platform finished at the café and there was no obvious way out. In those few seconds Nathan realised that there was only one choice for him. He threw the packet of sandwiches at the group as hard as he could, turned and jumped onto the rail track, running away from them in the direction of the Westside.

After a few seconds the four followed. Nathan could hear shouting from the station staff but he kept on running. Three of the group behind were clearly not as fit as Nathan, although the other one was managing to stay about twenty yards behind him. Nathan was thankful of all the time he had spent in the prison gym, thereby giving him that extra bit of stamina.

After what seemed an eternity, but could only have been several hundred yards, Nathan and the struggling pack behind reached the viaduct crossing the River Severn; this viaduct was at some considerable height, dwarfing Worcester's magnificent cathedral some distance below.

Nathan was about three-quarters across, with the lead person from the group about halfway across when a train came towards them from the direction of the station. Nathan quickly swung himself onto the top of the viaduct side barrier. The lead thug seemed to completely panic, throwing himself likewise onto the side barrier, but in his panic he completely lost his balance and tumbled over the edge down the deep drop into the river. In the past Nathan had seen local foolhardy lads jump from there into the river during hot summer days, but whether the person who had just fallen in survived or not, Nathan didn't care.

The other three in the pursuing group, who were more aware of the approaching train, quickly moved to the other side of the tracks to avoid it. Having seen their friend disappear over the edge of the bridge, they decided to cut their losses and retreat back to the station.

Ignoring the warning noises from the train, Nathan waited until it had passed and then continued over the bridge. After some distance he came to a level crossing where he moved off the rail track onto a footpath that ran beside the railway line, where he continued on his way further into the Westside.

CHAPTER 2

1992

It was the closing years of the Conservative Government and Thatcher had resigned as Prime Minister. There had been over a decade of the destruction of time honoured skills and professions, leading to high unemployment and protest. The hopes and vision of the 1960s had been crushed. A period of despair, lack of hope and direction for many young people ensued and some saw their future outside the established social order.

Life at home had been difficult for Nathan; his parents were constantly arguing, which wasn't helped by his father's insecure work situation and his elder brother wanted out. Nathan had finished Sixth Form College in 1990 and had decided to take a gap year before he took up a place at university.

It was around the time of leaving college that his friend Robbie suggested they joined a group of New-Age Travellers in Somerset. Nathan jumped at the chance to get away from home and 'live life' before university. Robbie could drive and had an old caravan, which they drove down to Somerset and there they met up with a small group of 'New-Age Travellers'.

It was here, in the spring of 1991, that Nathan met Rosalind. She was one or two years older and much more experienced than Nathan; a beautiful American woman with long auburn hair. The more the young Nathan saw of Rosalind, the more he became infatuated with her. The only thing that spoilt her appearance was her poor teeth. Nathan found this surprising, being led by the impression that all Americans seemed to imply that they all had good teeth, especially when compared to the British.

Nathan learnt that Rosalind had arrived from America for the Glastonbury Festival, joined up with a group of New Age Travellers and taken to the road with them, thereby avoiding the Immigration people.

Eventually he moved in with her, although life became difficult with her because as well as a free spirit, she had a serious drug problem. His infatuation was such that he was prepared to overlook anything and the relationship developed with Nathan making many concessions.

Surviving the winter in their flimsy vehicles, spring arrived the following year with the start of the Free Festival season. Nathan, Rosalind and Robbie, with the rest of their group of travellers, turned up for the Avon Free Festival. Unfortunately for them the police had managed to put a stop to it before it started.

The group then moved on to Gloucestershire, but after an aborted attempt to get onto Inglefield Common, where the police had found it easy to defend against an invasion, they received information via the 'Rave' telephone line, plus word of mouth, that there was to be a big event at Castlemorton in Worcestershire.

Unfortunately for the police in Worcestershire, events conspired against them, preventing any traveller invasion on Castlemorton Common. Their resources were tied up with a triple fatal accident on the M5, which created total chaos, plus police resources were called out to racial tension incidents in Frankley.

Nathan and his fellow group of travellers arrived at Castlemorton at about 7.00 p.m. on Friday 22nd May, the start of the Spring Bank Holiday, on what was to be the new site for the Spring Free Festival. Access onto the Common was easy because a B-road that led into Gloucestershire intersected it and entry onto to the Common itself was flat on either side of the road.

There were already at least one hundred assorted vehicles on the Common with news on the grapevine that there were hundreds more on the road heading that way from Wales, Somerset and other areas. Several thousand people were already there and apparently there was a mile-long queue of vehicles waiting to get onto the site.

By the next morning news of the event had spread like wildfire, with messages going out on underground radio and even on BBC Radio One, that there was a 'rave' party going on at Castlemorton Common. Due to the publicity the event took on a life of its own, leading to the ridiculous situation of 'Ravers' outnumbering 'New-Age Travellers' by three to one, with approximately 20,000 on site (5,000 New-Age Travellers and 15,000 'Ravers'). However, the 'Rave' community and New-Age Travellers weren't always necessary good bed companions.

With the rave community came the drug dealers, and

other detritus of criminals, who set up camp with a 'wagon-train' of vehicles around their operation. Also, muggers from Brixton arrived with their own bodyguards. L.S.D., cannabis, amphetamines and ecstasy were openly on sale and guns were on open show. The police could get nowhere near; all they could do was stay on the perimeter and try to contain it.

Marquees and stages were set up with at least five powerful sound systems. Anarchy ruled as groups such as 'Spiral Tribe' (an anagram for 'Bril Parties'), 'Circus War' and 'Bedlam' blasted out their music, along with the other sound systems, all day and night. 'The Exploding Gerbil' café set up a sign on the road, stating: 'Civilisation ends here. Drive slow or DIE!' which added to the general atmosphere of intimidation for local people or anyone else who dared to go near.

There were a number of isolated houses on the common and the residents soon appeared to be in some danger. A marked police car containing Council representatives tried to reach two elderly ladies in their eighties, who lived in an isolated cottage on the Common, but had to get out quickly after the car was kicked and dented, with threats made to overturn and attack it with a chainsaw.

Many visitors to the site were held up at knifepoint and made to turn out their pockets. A Roger Cook TV crew trying to film the events was attacked and one reporter received a broken shoulder. Also many of the isolated cottages on the Common were broken into and flares were fired at police helicopters as they hovered overhead.

Nathan was beginning to find all this totally

overwhelming and in some ways would have preferred to leave. However Rosalind was totally in her element, dancing bare-footed around the Common, her long hair flowing with her dance movements.

Although Nathan was happy enough to partake in many of the more soft drugs available, the whole out of control drug scene was to lead to disaster for him. Rosalind, with her drug habits, was totally at ease with everything and soon became high on whatever she could obtain. It was during this period that they came into contact with the Grivens brothers, Dwayne and Darren. In many ways they were small-time dealers, but they weren't particular on how they gained their profits, getting involved with not just heavy drug dealing, but also in the mugging and robbery that was also taking place.

Rosalind was quite happy to buy whatever she wanted from them. One minute high, stimulated by the continuous blasting music and drugs, and the next in a drug-induced stupor. This worried Nathan; he felt he needed to protect her, but she was such a free soul that he felt powerless and as a consequence frustrated and angry.

He wondered how she paid for the drugs. He was aware that she had access to some family money, but he worried that this wouldn't last forever. He guessed that in her early days of addiction the drugs would probably have been given to her to get her addicted, but it certainly would not have been the case now that she was addicted. He just hoped that she wasn't doing anything else illegal to pay for them.

The 'rave' continued the next day, Sunday and into

Monday. By then the whole area began to stink; there were no toilet facilities and whilst the travellers made attempts to bury their excrement, the 'ravers' were totally unconcerned. The problems were made worse due to the first effects of ecstasy use leading to a loosening of the bowels.

Although Nathan had enjoyed the quieter aspect of the traveller lifestyle over the winter and early spring months, mainly because of his obsession with Rosalind, he however, resented the fact that the atmosphere of the rave was a distraction for Rosalind from his affections. He also found the violent atmosphere of the rave not to his liking and wanted to leave. Robbie was of the same view too, but he, like Nathan, had taken up with a woman of the name of Angie and she, like Rosalind, was enjoying the danger of the whole experience.

Over the weekend Nathan had watched with irritated patience as Darren Grivens paid visits to Rosalind in her trailer, dishing out drugs to her. As the days went by Nathan grew to despise Grivens and wished him dead.

On the Tuesday afternoon he watched again as Darren Grivens entered Rosalind's vehicle. Feeling frustrated and angry he walked to the outskirts of the Common. He hadn't analysed it before, but it began to dawn on him that regardless of his parents' differences, he had been brought up a law abiding person and this began to reflect in his feelings of revulsion about the whole spectacle over the last few days. He felt soured by the whole 'New-Age' experience. The squalor of the situation was beginning to sicken him.

He glanced out over the Common, remembering his familiarity with this bleak stretch of moorland-type common land. He had first visited the area on a school natural sciences trip to study the anthills and was struck by its bleak beauty, set against a backcloth of the magnificent Malvern Hills that seemed to spring out of the ground a mile or so away. As a boy, in his own time, he had cycled out to the Common and sat fascinated for many an hour watching the green woodpeckers feed ferociously from the tops of the anthills.

Looking around, he sighed, remembering it as it was; a place of serenity and haunting beauty. Seeing this area now, this S.S.S.I., he felt ashamed and unclean. At that moment his thoughts were interrupted by a couple of mad 'ravers' tearing past him on quad bikes, obliterating the surface of the Common.

Many people were now starting to drift away from the site. Nathan saw this as a good opportunity to persuade Rosalind to move away from the Common to a quieter encampment where they could be together. Encouraged by these thoughts, he walked back to Rosalind's trailer.

As he entered he sensed that something was wrong. Rosalind lay senseless on the bed and by her side was the needle that she had used. Also on the bed was an assortment of pills and an empty bottle of vodka. Her dress had been lifted up and her pants were cast aside on the floor. It clearly looked to him that she had been raped. He looked at her, she didn't appear to be breathing and his heart sank. Panic arose in his stomach and chest. Bending down to her, he lifted her into a sitting position, shook her and shouted hysterically at her. There was no response. Placing her back down, he ran to Robbie's caravan, practically screaming at Robbie and Angie.

'She's dead, she's dead!' he screeched. 'That bastard, he's killed her!'

Robbie and Angie stared at him in shocked amazement.

Nathan began to sweat profusely and his mind began to cloud over. He felt irrational and not in control of his emotions. Grabbing a knife on the side that Robbie had kept for protection, Nathan charged out of the caravan and ran like a demented demon through the diminishing crowd looking for Darren Grivens.

A hundred yards ahead he could see the Grivens' vehicle on the road behind a queue leaving the Common. Running like a madman he reached the vehicle before it had covered any distance. Tearing at the door on the passenger side he reached inside and pulled at Grivens. Not wearing a seatbelt, he fell out of the car with ease.

'You bastard, you bastard!' Nathan screamed, and plunged the knife into Grivens a number of times.

Being near the edge of the Common the police had full view of the incident and were quickly upon the scene, leading to Nathan being quickly restrained.

A police officer knelt down and examined Grivens; looking up, he shook his head. 'He's dead!' he exclaimed.

Dwayne Grivens had already scrambled out of the driving seat and was rounding the car. 'You cunt!' he yelled. 'I'll get you for this!'

Several police officers held him back as Nathan was led away.

CHAPTER 3

ROBBIE'S DILEMMA

It took Nathan another half an hour to reach Robbie's house on the outskirts of Worcester's Westside. He felt he owed Robbie a lot; whilst back in 1992, when he was ruining his life and putting himself in danger with his impulsive actions, Robbie had acted calmly and responsibly. After Nathan had dashed out, stating that Rosalind was dead, Robbie had gone straight to Rosalind's trailer. Seeing Rosalind lay there, he also began to panic a little, however on examining her and seeing what he thought to be some very faint sign of life, he carried her to his car and drove furiously to the nearest hospital. After spending some weeks in a coma, Rosalind eventually recovered consciousness.

Whilst on remand, awaiting trial, Robbie was able to inform Nathan that Rosalind was alive and in a coma. On later visits he updated him on Rosalind regaining consciousness from the coma and the time she had spent in hospital receiving treatment. Robbie could visibly see for himself, that with this information it helped lift Nathan out of depression and despair, enabling him to accept his time in prison more.

Nathan firmly believed that it was Robbie's prompt action that saved Rosalind's life, giving him a reason to live and accept the next twenty-three years. The thoughts that he would one day get out and be with Rosalind kept him alive physically and mentally. He wrote letter after letter to Rosalind and although he never received a reply of any kind, the writing became part of his journey, the feelings in his mind that kept him going.

Although Robbie had only been able to visit him about once a year, preferring instead to write, he never appeared to want to talk too much about Rosalind, however he repeated that she, as far as he was aware, was well. After watching the feelings of joy that came to Nathan's face, Robbie always cut the conversation short, however, by saying that he had lost contact with her and couldn't tell Nathan any more than that she was alive and seemed to be doing okay.

Nathan hadn't informed Robbie that he intended to visit him today, but he was anxious to be filled in with the latest situation. In his many letters to Nathan, Robbie had told him that after Castlemorton and Nathan's imprisonment, he and Angie had spent several years on the road, working on the land, picking crops to earn money. At that time Angie became pregnant, so tired of the hard life outside, they decided to settle down and get married. Robbie had told him that he'd then got a job in Social Care looking after adults with a learning disability in the community. Since then, over the next ten years they'd had two more children. All this, the intervening years; Robbie, Angie and their children; and especially news of Rosalind, Nathan was anxious to catch up on.

Arriving at the address he knew from Robbie's letters, he knocked and Angie answered the door.

They stood there looking at one another for what seemed minutes, but could only have been seconds. Certainly, Angie initially looked puzzled and then slowly she began to recognise him. It was slightly similar for Nathan. Angie had gained a little weight and was fuller-faced, but still looked the attractive woman he had know twenty-three years previously. But perhaps what was most noticeable and surprising for Nathan was that she appeared to be very pregnant.

'Nathan!' gasped Angie. 'But we weren't expecting you.' Turning round, she shouted into the house, 'Rob, you'll never guess, it's Nathan.'

Robbie came to the door rather gingerly. He smiled on seeing Nathan. 'Hi mate, nice to see you,' he said, hugging Nathan. 'Why didn't you tell us you were coming? Come on in, we probably need to talk.'

'Hey, you've put on a bit of muscle,' said Angie, nodding towards his shoulders and biceps.

'Yeah,' replied Nathan, looking a little embarrassed. 'There's not much to do in prison and working out in the gym helps kill the time.'

Robbie and Angie's living room was sparsely furnished, although very clean, with what seemed second-hand furniture, none of it seeming to match. The picture it painted was of a family that was struggling.

'I think the first thing I'd better say to you both is congratulations,' said Nathan, smiling at them.

'Oh that,' smiled Robbie, grudgingly. 'It was, as they say, rather unexpected.'

They sat down and for a several seconds there was an uncomfortable silence, which was then interrupted by Nathan.

'You must tell me everything that's gone on,' he said with enthusiasm. 'Have you still got that job as a care worker?'

'Well, no,' grimaced Robbie. 'You see, the job was to support people with a learning disability integrate and live normally in the community. Well at least that's the theory that goes along with the job and policy. The reality of it is that the money is crap, there's no money to help anyone, and vulnerable people such as these just become the bottom level of exploitation in the community. People who think up these theories don't understand the structures of the poor. But the set-up I worked for lost the contract so I was out of a job. Anyway with the frustrations of the job and the money I was glad in some ways to get out of it. I thought perhaps I'd be better off on the dole.'

'And are you?' questioned Nathan.

'Well not really,' replied Robbie. 'But I'm no worse off in a way because most of the jobs now seem to be zero hours; total exploitation. We now have to rely on the food bank mainly to feed us and the kids. Life is shit. I'm still looking for some kind of work, but it's difficult. But at the moment, at least, I suppose I can spend more time in bed,' he joked.

'It looks like it,' grinned Nathan, glancing at Angie's bulge.

'Yeah if he'd kept his job we might not have got ourselves into this,' sighed Angie. 'But never mind, we shall do our best.'

'Look,' said Nathan, deciding to change the subject, 'I know you always told me that you have had no contact with Rosalind, but I'm desperate to know the latest situation. What can you tell me?'

There was a pause from the other two. Robbie looked at Angie and she shrugged her shoulders.

'You'll have to tell him,' she said.

'Tell me what?' questioned Nathan.

At that moment a banging at the door interrupted the awkwardness of the situation. Angie rose up, walked to the door and opened it. In rushed three noisy children, a girl and two boys, of various ages ranging from about six to ten.

'School's finished, peace over,' stated Robbie.

The children froze for a moment on seeing Nathan.

'It's all right, he won't bite,' said Robbie. 'It's Nathan, an old mate. Just take no notice of him.'

The children ignored Nathan, dropped an assortment of papers and paintings into Angie's lap, and continued on their journey towards the kitchen. This was followed by the sound of cupboards and fridge doors opening.

'Don't get eating too much,' shouted Angie. 'You won't want your tea.' Turning to Nathan she explained, 'They're so ravenous when they get back. I don't know whether they don't eat their school dinners or they don't get much.'

'They're growing fast, I dare say,' said Nathan.

At that the children came in munching an assortment of crisps and biscuits, and slumped into chairs.

'Good day at school?' asked Robbie.

The children just nodded back, their mouths full.

'Anyway, as we were saying,' said Nathan. 'What can you tell me about Rosalind?'

Robbie looked serious, stared at the ground for a few moments, and then looking up he said, 'Look Nathan, there's something you should really know about Ros, er, Rosalind. You know I told you she was in a coma for some weeks, which she eventually came round from. Well perhaps I wasn't being one hundred percent honest with you when I said I thought she was okay. The truth is she came out of the coma with an acquired brain injury. She will never be the same person again that you knew.'

'What do you mean, acquired brain injury?' demanded a desperate Nathan. 'You must tell me. I really need to know. I must see her.'

'Look Nathan, she will never be the same again,' replied Robbie, trying to remain calm and supportive.

'FUCK-ING HELL, Robbie!' stormed Nathan.

'NATHAN!' shouted Robbie, interrupting him. 'Watch the ham sandwich! I know a lot of kids are familiar with words like that, but we try to protect our kids. It's not easy.'

'Yes,' interjected Angie, agreeing with Robbie.

'I'm sorry,' whispered Nathan. 'But it was a shock.'

'I'm afraid it's true,' returned Robbie. 'I'm afraid

she's no longer the person you knew. Although I haven't seen her since that night. I can only guess, to put it crudely, that she's no longer the ticket.'

'Tell me, how is she now? Surely she will need me now more than ever?' whimpered Nathan.

'Look mate, I honestly don't know. I haven't seen her, as I said, since that night,' replied an exasperated Robbie. 'However, there is one other piece of information you will need to know.'

At that stage Robbie looked at Angie, seeking support. She screwed up her face and shrugged her shoulders.

'Well it's like this,' continued Robbie. 'Ros got married a few years later.'

'Oh no!' gasped Nathan, clamping his hands to his face. 'Oh, no, no, no, NO!' His voice rose as he spoke, the volume of which startled the children.

Seeing this, Angie rose up from her chair and said to the children, 'Go and play in your bedroom for a little,' ushering them out of the room. 'We won't be long.' Then turning to Nathan she said, 'I'm afraid they all have to share the same bedroom, which isn't ideal.'

There followed a difficult silence. A worried Robbie looked at Angie and she returned with a similar expression of helpless concern.

After what could only have been a minute, but seemed much longer, Nathan broke the silence. 'Who to? Who was it?' he asked bluntly.

'As far as I can make out,' Robbie started to explain, 'there was this young copper who was given the job of keeping an eye on her in hospital, probably to possibly find out more about what happened to her and whether it had any connections to your actions. Although, she couldn't remember a thing. Anyway it seems he must have taken a shine to her and started to visit her socially and when she was eventually discharged he volunteered the role of acting as a carer for her. It sort of went on from there. I suppose as an American citizen and disabled she was in a vulnerable position. Look Nathan, I'm sorry, I just couldn't tell you any of this; I knew how you felt about her and the way you reacted when you heard she was alive. It just seemed cruel to crush you further. You've got to agree the thoughts of her kept you going, without that, I've no doubt you would have crumbled psychologically.'

Nathan stared blankly for some moments. 'What am I going to do?' he asked despairingly. After a short silence he continued in a more decisive manner. 'This is a mess. I think I will have to leave the area.'

'What makes you say that?' asked Robbie.

Nathan told him about the reception he'd received when he got off the train.

'I don't think I can go to the hostel now, they'll know where I am and that will be that,' said Nathan pessimistically.

'Look, Nathan,' said Robbie. 'Why don't you phone the hostel and explain what happened and ask if you can perhaps stay with us overnight?' Robbie looked at Angie and mouthed silently to her, 'Is that all right?'

Angie shrugged her shoulders in resignation.

'We haven't got a spare bed,' continued Robbie, 'but you can kip down on the settee tonight and then perhaps we can sort something out with your Parole Officer tomorrow. But you need to speak to them, I'm sure they will understand, otherwise if you don't they will think you've gone walkabout.'

Nathan phoned the hostel and reached an agreement with them about staying overnight with Robbie. They then settled down for the evening.

After an evening meal and when the children were all in bed, Robbie suggested that he might be able to arrange alternative accommodation to the hostel for him.

'Jack Armstrong, you know him Angie don't you?'

Angie nodded.

'Jack helped us get this place when he was a councillor, as you can see it's a bit crap, although I suppose he did his best. The private landlord only seems interested in his rent and nothing much else. Thank God we get Housing Benefit otherwise we would never be able to afford it. You can't get social housing now for love or money,' continued Robbie. 'Anyway, Jack's wife died a few years ago and since then he's taken in selective lodgers. He may well consider you, after all didn't he know your father?'

Nathan thought for a few seconds. 'Yeah, I vaguely remember him,' he replied. 'I think they either worked together or were on the local Trades Union Council together, something like that.'

'He'll probably bore the pants off you with his Socialist rants, but he's got a heart of gold,' said Robbie.

Robbie phoned and Jack responded by suggesting that Nathan visited him the next day after discussing the matter with the Parole Officer.

That evening they settled down with numerous cups of tea and biscuits, recounting the past. Nathan relaxed more as the evening went on, as they got high on tales of their exploits as young people, although it seemed noticeable to Robbie and Angie that Nathan occasionally dropped into periods of depression.

At bedtime that night, Robbie turned to Angie in bed and said, 'You know, he ain't going to let it drop is he? Being locked up for over twenty years, no women, just obsessively thinking about one woman, it's got to affect you somehow.' Then changing the tone he said, chuckling, 'What he needs is a good woman. Do you know any?'

'No. Fuck off and go to sleep,' Angie drowsily replied.

Robbie laughed, kissed Angie, and turned over.

'I still say we haven't heard the end of this yet,' Robbie mumbled into his pillow. 'He just ain't going to let it drop.'

CHAPTER 4

JACK ARMSTRONG

'I knew your dad. A bloody good Socialist,' said Jack Armstrong, showing Nathan into his front room. Jack had the appearance of an ageing street fighter, a wiry, white-haired person in his sixties, who looked, precisely as Robbie had described to Nathan, as if he'd had plenty of personal battles of own, as well as public battles with employers and authorities. 'So it's okay for you to stay here then?' asked Jack.

'Yeah,' replied Nathan. 'The Parole Officer, or whatever he was, said he knew of you and seemed to think it might be an appropriate place to stay.'

'He did, did he?' replied a deadpan Jack. 'Well I've taken some in from the past that Probation have passed on to me. Some have bin a bloody nuisance and I was thinking that I won't do it anymore, but as I said I knew your dad. We were on Trades Council together. So, for his sake alone, I'll give you a chance.'

'Thanks,' replied a grateful Nathan. Anything was better than a hostel with other crims, he thought.

'Yeah,' continued Jack, directing Nathan to a well-worn armchair to sit in. 'I remember your case well. The whole thing devastated your dad,' he said solemnly. 'I reckon you had a raw deal then. Useless bastards like that have it coming. No bugger sheds a tear over people like that.' There was a few moments' silence as Jack stared at the wall in deep thought. Snapping out of the mood in a more lively fashion, he continued: 'But anyway, the world's got to be a better place since you got rid of that scum. It's only a pity that you had to spend so much time in prison for it. So what's you gonna do now you're out? Get a job? That'll be bloody difficult I bet.'

'Yeah, I know,' replied Nathan. 'I'd never worked before I went inside. I've got no trade, so I don't know what I'll do. Although I did manage to take a degree inside prison.'

'Well nobody much has got a trade nowadays,' replied Jack bluntly. 'It seems it's all mainly crap unskilled work now. It seems most people end up in call centres being abused by the public that call. Your dad was made redundant after many years as a skilled worker in the print trade; new technology you know. So what with unemployment, which led to his ongoing problems with depression, I don't think that helped things much at home with your mam. He was a good bloke though, a good friend,' he continued thoughtfully. 'You know, he got a silver badge from the Maerdy miners for the money he'd collected for them during the '84 strike, as well as the money his Union had collected for them.'

'Yeah, I remember,' said Nathan. 'I remember we all went to Maerdy in a coach to visit during the strike. I couldn't have been more than ten or eleven.'

'Yeah, I remember you lad,' said Jack. 'Yes, that trip was organised by your dad's print union you know. I remember it well, particularly because of the financial situation of many of the miners the union advised us to take our own food and eat it before we got off the coach. It was generally felt that we didn't want to be imposing on the miners, eating their food, when they had very little themselves.'

'Yeah,' responded Nathan enthusiastically. 'But when we got off the coach and went into the Community Hall, we were amazed to find that they'd sacrificed their valuable food supplies to put on a great spread for us.'

'That's right,' said Jack. 'They must have been very proud people, good people. You know I cried like a babby when I saw them on the tele, marching back proudly to the pit when the strike was called off.'

'It was a good day, that trip to Maerdy,' said a thoughtful Nathan. 'Good experience, especially when they took us down the mine. I remember some of the other kids that came with us got frightened and started to cry, but I was okay.'

'I bet you were,' laughed Jack. 'Anyway, I'll show you your room. I have a simple breakfast; toast or cereals, so you can have some of that. But you'll have to sort out the rest of your own meals yourself. I'm not much of a cook, although sometimes I've managed to knock something up at night if the person staying helps.'

'Well I'll help as much as I can,' said Nathan.

'Thanks,' replied Jack. 'However, you'll find I have most of my meals in the pub.'

'You still a Councillor?' asked Nathan. 'Rob told me you helped them get their house.'

'Na,' replied Jack, looking serious. 'Bloody New Labour, I refused to toe the "New" Labour, Blair line. In my opinion it wasn't Socialism, just pinching and adding to the name of a proud party. I tried going it alone, but it's difficult without the party machine behind you.'

'Well everything looks fine here to me,' said Nathan, interrupting Jack's thoughts to change the subject. 'However, I need to get some clothes, I've only got what I stand up in. The Probation gave me a letter to take to a charity to get some clothes.'

'Yeah, I know it,' said Jack. 'It's just down the road. They do some good work.'

At that point there was a knock at the door. Jack went to the front door and brought in Robbie.

'Yer mate's come to see you,' said Jack.

'Aye, I've been to the Job Centre for an interview, so I thought I'd call and see how things were going,' said Robbie.

'Fine,' replied Jack. 'But what's this about signing on? I thought you had a job?'

'Yeah, I did,' replied Robbie. 'But the situation was driving me mad, so I jacked it in.'

'So another idol bugger, living off benefit, hey?' retorted Jack.

'I guess so. But what would you do?' responded Robbie.

'Oy,' resigned Jack, 'I feel really sorry for young people now. When I was young we had apprenticeships and young lads were trained to become skilled tradesmen. Now what have we got?

33

Bugger all! Bloody new technology, it's only there in the end to benefit the bleeding capitalists.'

'You know,' continued Robbie, 'I was stood waiting to be seen at the Job Centre, and there was this young lad in front, who from the way he was talking had just come out of prison. He was saying "Fuck this for a lark. When I was inside I had four square meals a day and nothing else to worry about. I don't think I'll stay out here wasting my time much longer".'

'Have you got a car?' Nathan asked Jack, suddenly changing the direction of the conversation which was beginning to irritate him, startling the other two.

'Yes, why?' asked a puzzled Jack.

'It's just that I need to visit Castlemorton,' replied Nathan. 'I need to get things right in my head.'

Robbie sighed internally and shut his eyes for a few seconds. After the previous night he'd thought Nathan was accepting things and getting over his obsession with Rosalind, but perhaps he was asking too much, he thought. Perhaps Nathan just needed to work things through in his head.

'You cheeky bugger!' retorted Jack to Nathan's request. He thought for a few moments and then responded in a less aggravated tone. 'Yes, well just about, but I don't know how long I can afford to keep it going.' There was a few seconds' silence, where Jack appeared to be thinking. 'Well yes, I suppose I could take you there. The Malvern's and Castlemorton area were favourite places for me and my missus when she was alive.' There was another silence as Jack stared into space. 'She was a good'un,' he continued. 'You don't get many like her.' Then suddenly lightening the mood he said, 'Hey there's a pub on the Common, perhaps we can go there for a drink. I think I might be owed one or two.'

The others laughed.

CHAPTER 5

THE COPPER

'It's fucking hell out there,' stormed a dripping wet PC Roger Gwillam to his colleague PC Dave Barnes, as they stood in the police station locker room. 'Look, some bastard has spewed down my trousers and on my shoe,' he continued, pointing downwards and raising his leg in Dave's direction.

Dave and Roger had just returned to the police station from policing night club revellers as they left the clubs in the early hours, hustling one another for taxis and fast food. Having broken up a drunken fight, Dave and Roger had brought in a particularly nasty customer, who seemed high as a kite on some substance or another, to be charged for assault.

'Well, thank goodness, at least I've got tomorrow off and then I'm back on early duty,' said Dave Barnes, issuing a deep relaxed sigh.

'Yeah, me too. At least you're dealing with more normal people in the daytime,' replied a jaundiced Roger.

'Well fairly normal,' chuckled Dave.

Roger gave a knowing smile.

Pulling a clean pair of trousers out of his locker,

Roger proceeded to change. 'What's Ros doing tonight? Is anyone with her?' he asked Dave.

'My mother's staying with her tonight,' replied Dave. 'She's been okay on her own now for years but I just don't want to take the chance. She seems to be able to do most things and go most places on her own, mostly without difficulty, but perhaps I'm just rather overprotective. Although she's a lot better than she was years ago, I do worry about her whenever she goes out. Her speech, co-ordination and mobility are not perfect, and on odd occasions she can still get confused, leading to her forgetting where she is and wandering off. However, her fits seem to have lessened considerably. She hasn't had one now for some time.'

'It can't be easy being a carer and doing a job like this,' stated Roger, pulling on his trousers.

'It's bloody difficult,' replied Dave. 'But I need to work, otherwise things would get even more difficult on the finance front. I suppose it's my own choice, but caring for someone like Ros is a commitment for life, although I've never regretted my decision to marry her.'

'Brave lad,' said Roger. 'A little different from that bastard tonight. A useless member of society. He's taken an assortment of drink and drugs, causes chaos, won't remember a thing in the morning and probably all he'll get is a bleeding fine. What the fuck do we do this job for? It can't be for the money.'

'You make a relevant point,' replied a thoughtful Dave.

Roger looked at Dave, as if to check how he was

and then asked, 'Did you know Nathan Hancock was released the other day. Do you think he'll try to see Ros?'

'Yes, I'd heard on the grapevine,' replied Dave, looking serious. 'I don't know, I hope not. I really don't want her being reminded of all that went on all those years ago, particularly the drug difficulties. It was some time before we managed to get her clean of drugs, but now, hopefully without any interference from her past, then she should be all right. After all she's been clean now for a long time and due to her condition she's not likely to mix with anyone who can lead her back down that route. So you can see why I may be anxious about anyone from her past turning up now.'

'I hear there was some trouble at the railway station. Do you think he was involved?' asked Roger.

'It's likely,' replied Dave. 'That yob they fished out of the Severn was a known associate of Dwayne Grivens, so one can guess that Hancock was probably the target.'

'Yes,' interrupted Roger. That guy was lucky there were some fishermen nearby who fished him out, otherwise he'd probably have drowned.'

'It's amazing, incidents like that and you can never directly point a finger at Grivens, but everyone knows he's got to be at the back of it all,' said Dave.

'You bet,' replied Roger. 'But try proving it. He seems to tie up every aspect of his time with so-called alibis. He must have a brain on him for a nasty bastard. Have you seen his house, just outside Malvern? He must be making a fortune or something.'

'I suppose he'd argue that he's made his money from the tacky goods he has in his warehouse. Not a bad front for drugs,' said Dave.

'It makes you sick,' continued Roger, putting on his shoes. 'We do a job like this and all it involves without a great reward and cunts like that fuck up every decent thing we believe in.'

'What do you think the chances are of Hancock showing up, trying to see Rosalind?' asked Dave, beginning to look worried.

'Your guess is as good as mine,' replied Roger. 'But he's going to have to watch himself. One false move and I'm sure we can drop a word to Probation. That'll slow him down, I'm sure.'

CHAPTER 6

THE COMMON

'I don't know what you can see in this place,' remarked a jaundiced Robbie, waving his arms in either direction as they wandered about the bleak, deserted area of Castlemorton Common, trying to avoid sodden areas of ground.

'I needed to get here and revisit the past,' replied a sombre but determined Nathan. 'This is where it all happened for me, where my life was shattered. You've got to remember I lost my freedom here, twenty-three bloody years of my life, and perhaps most importantly this is where I lost the love of my life.'

'Come on Rob, surely you can see the raw beauty of this place,' interjected Jack, trying to change the rather dismal atmosphere that had pervaded over the threesome.

'You don't know what it's like Robbie, being shut up for year upon year,' explained Nathan. 'You have to have something to keep you going; a dream, otherwise your life would be completely hell. My dream was to return here with Rosalind. This was what kept me alive, day after day, night after night. I couldn't completely descend into my hell when my heaven gave me some will to live.'

'Yeah, that I understand,' replied Robbie in a less confrontational tone.

Jack, irritated by the other two and their rather sombre mood, suddenly stopped walking and lifted up his head, breathing in the air. 'You know what?' he said, staring around him, hoping to change the atmosphere. 'This place, the location, particularly the road, reminds me of that scene from Hitchcock's "North by North-West". You know the scene where Cary Grant gets off a bus, or whatever it was, and walks down the road, just before he is pursued by the crop-spraying aircraft into the field of maize. Of course this is nothing like that area in lots of ways, this landscape's a lot greener than that in the film, but there is an atmosphere in the Hitchcock film that you feel here. Can anybody see it, feel it?'

'Yeah,' responded Nathan brightly, as if a major idea had just struck him. 'Yeah, that's where I've seen it before. It's always bugged me seeing this place, the road, not being able to place it and now I know. Thanks Jack,' he said, smiling widely at him.

'I don't know what the hell you're on about,' groaned Robbie. 'I just don't see it.'

'Well, I suppose we all see things differently,' answered a more sombre Nathan. 'But anyway, as I said before, I had my dream, my heaven. We all have to have our dreams, our own personal heavens.'

'Come on you two,' said Jack, trying to change the mood. 'All this talk of heaven, let's get across the Common to the pub – my heaven, and have a pint or two.'

Jack's remarks lightened the atmosphere and the

other two chuckled as they made their way towards the pub.

Walking onto the road, which ran through the Common, Robbie sensed the need to loosen the atmosphere further by telling a dirty joke. He'd just about got to the punch line when a car drove up beside them.

In the car were two men. Driving slowly by the side of the threesome, the windows of the car began to wind down and a thuggish-looking man stuck his head out of the window. Nathan recognised him as one of his reception committee at the station two days previous.

The man smiled sardonically. 'Nice to see you Hand-cock,' he said sarcastically. 'Just to let you know we're watching you.'

'You're goin' to be pigmeat mate!' shouted the other man from the driver's seat.

Then they both burst out laughing in a hysterical, childish fashion. 'Yea, pigmeat. Oink, oink, snork, snork,' the men spluttered out between bouts of hysterical laughter.

With these chilling words they accelerated away from them. The three watched as the car disappeared down the road into the distance.

'NATHAN!' said Robbie, his voice rising to a shout. 'They must have followed us here. It looks like Grivens is onto you. You're going to have to watch your every step.'

'Bastards!' stormed Jack. 'Do you think it's safe for you to stay living in the area, Nathan?'

'I've not done yet. I still have things to do,' replied

Nathan. 'If I'm ever going to sort out my head then I've got to sort things out further. I can't leave this area without getting things straight with Rosalind.'

'For fuck's sake!' stormed Robbie. 'You can't torture yourself like this. She's married and perhaps more relevantly she's got a disability, which means she may not even remember you.'

'You don't know that,' Nathan snarled back. 'I've got to see her. There's no other answer. I can't just shut her out of my mind.'

Jack sighed at the other two arguing. He stopped suddenly, turned around slowly to get a panoramic view of the countryside, then stopping for a few moments in a thoughtful mode, he breathed in the air deeply, his actions silencing the other two.

'You know,' he said to the two. 'You look around at this scenery and then look at the scum we just saw. What do you see? Beauty,' waving his arm across the Common towards the Malvern Hills. 'And the beast,' waving his arm in the direction the car had gone. 'This is a beautiful country and this is a particularly beautiful area. I love this country, so we just can't let the scum – the beast – taint the beauty.'

The other two noticed at that stage that Jack's eyes were starting to moisten.

Then suddenly becoming aware of his emotional condition, Jack decided to change the mood. He turned abruptly to the other two and said in an upbeat tone, 'For Christ's sake, let's have that drink. My tongue's hanging out; these things will have to be sorted out later. But for goodness' sake let's have a drink, you owe me one at least.'

CHAPTER 7

THE BUSINESS

Lump, a gangling man in his early twenties, sat slumped in a tatty armchair in Dwayne Grivens' warehouse office. With no coat, just jeans and a tee-shirt on top, he exposed an expanse of tattoos down his arms and around his neck. On his left eyebrow he had a stud piercing.

As Dwayne Grivens walked into the room, Lump immediately straightened himself upright in the chair, not so much out of genuine respect, more respect through fear. He, like Grivens' other henchmen, would have been users as well as pushers of drugs. Grivens knew that he gained loyalty from them when they too had some addiction to the drugs he provided; as well as their loyalty from fear.

Grivens eyed him up and down disdainfully as he walked into the room. 'Back with us after your ducking are you? What the fuck were you and the others messing at? Four of you and that bastard makes a monkey out of you. I've told you all, you're not here just for the distribution of the gear, your main job at the moment is the get him to me. I just wanna see his face when I smash him with the hammer. I want to see him scream, begging me for mercy. Have yer got it?'

'Sure boss and we almost had him,' squirmed Lump. 'Kev put the frighteners on him yesterday over on Castlemorton. It's just a matter of time before we can get him alone. He had two others with him so they couldn't do any more than put the shits up him.'

'That's right,' snarled Grivens, with an obsessional glint in his eyes. 'I don't want any witnesses. There's no way that I can be linked openly with what I've lined up for him, not with my business associations. I owe him, not just for what he did to my brother, but for the problems he caused me in what he said to the police at the time. Those bastards have been on my back ever since. I can't have them associating anything that happens to him through to me. Get it?'

'Sure, okay I get the message,' responded Lump, moving nervously towards the door.

'Well fuck off and get the bastard,' Grivens retorted. 'Earn your money you wanker. I want this sorted out pronto. Ali is delivering me a large consignment of cheap plastic toys, which should be packed with the works from the Middle East. With this consignment I intend to spread the business over the West Midlands. This could be my retirement package. There's a recession on and I want to get out before the punters start running out of money. Now get out, I've got warehouse business to concentrate on.'

As Lump moved further towards the door, Grivens continued as if as an after thought, 'Just remember, this consignment is strictly hush-hush. We can't afford another police raid. We've managed to get stuff off the premises quickly enough in the past for them to get pissed off, raiding the place and only finding the usual cheap crap we store here. So I will need you and the others here as soon as I get the delivery to move the stuff to your usual hideouts.'

CHAPTER 8

ROSALIND

Desire, attraction, passion, love, whatever you want to call it, Nathan's feelings for Rosalind had over the years grown into an obsession that had kept his spirit and mind together on those many long days and nights inside prison, and now that he was out the obsession was becoming uncontrollable. Rather like a blinkered animal led by its reins in a set direction.

Although Robbie had been reluctant to give Nathan Rosalind's address, he'd inadvertently, through conversations, given Nathan an indication of the area she was living in, which appeared to be the Westside, also details of her married name. All Nathan then had to do was the simple detection work of finding the actual full address through the telephone directory and from a copy of the electoral roll in the library.

That morning Nathan rose early and caught the bus to the Westside. He was working on the assumption that that Grivens' thugs would not be around that time in the morning, when most normal people went to work, and he was proved right.

Arriving at the location, he took the precaution of checking he'd got the right people at the right address by asking at the next door neighbour on the pretence that he'd believed that to be the address.

A woman in her thirties came to the door carrying a baby. Nathan asked, fully knowing that he didn't, whether PC Dave Barnes lived there.

'Oh, no,' replied the woman. 'He lives next door.'

'Do you know if he's in?' asked Nathan.

'No, I don't think so,' said the woman, starting to look puzzled. 'I thought I saw him go off on duty.'

'Oh well, perhaps Ros, Rosalind is in,' replied Nathan, hoping to reduce the woman's apparent puzzled unease.

However, the woman didn't respond.

Nathan thanked her and walked back onto the street, leaving the woman to stare suspiciously after him as she slowly closed the door.

At last, thought Nathan. *I'm so close now, so close.* With that thought he could almost hear his heart pound in his chest with excited anticipation and he was conscious that the palms of his hands were sweating profusely.

Cautiously, he slowly walked up the drive of the house. Standing for a few seconds, he wiped the sweat from his hands down the back of his jeans and then rang the doorbell.

There was no response, so he rang again. This time he heard the faltering footsteps of someone walking to the door.

The door opened and Rosalind stood in the entrance. Nathan had imagined and imagined in his mind over the years Rosalind's image, but seeing her now, it was as if in his mind the whole doorway entrance lit up. He was instantly aware of how clean her teeth were now and it dawned on him that she must have some dental work done. In his innocence he'd found out whilst in prison that serious drug use, particularly with heroin, rotted the teeth.

She had clearly aged a little but time had not diminished her beauty as Nathan saw it. Her hair was still the beautiful shade of auburn and although not so long as when he'd last seen her, it was still of a length to extend just down past her shoulders.

Now that he saw her he became speechless, unable to say anything. Rosalind stared at him, waiting for him to say something. A puzzled look came over her face.

'What do you want?' she said with a noticeable slur to her voice.

'Ra, Ros, Ros, it's, it's me, Nathan. Don't you recognise me? It's been a long, long time, but please say you recognise me.'

'Na-thon?' replied Rosalind, looking puzzled and narrowing her eyes as if to recognise someone through a thick fog. 'Is it you? I think I remember. It's so long ago.'

'Are you alone?' asked Nathan.

'Yeah, yes,' replied Rosalind, the words tumbling out of her mouth.

'Can I come in and talk to you? I really need to talk to you after all these years,' asked Nathan.

Rosalind hesitated for a few seconds. She then

turned and very slowly walked, with a slight limp to her left leg, down the hallway and turned to go through a doorway. Hesitating again, she waited for Nathan to follow and then continued into the lounge.

Nathan glanced behind and around him before entering and then followed, closing the front door behind him.

Rosalind sat down awkwardly into an armchair and Nathan followed by sitting in a chair opposite her.

There was a silence whilst they looked at one another. A look still of puzzlement on Rosalind's face and sublime bliss on Nathan's.

Nathan smiled warmly at her. 'How are you?' he asked gently. 'I know you have a disability.' But without waiting for an answer he continued. 'I've been away a long time.' Then looking at her to see any possible reaction he said quietly, 'In prison.' There was a short silence. 'You remember me from Castlemorton, please say you do,' he said pleadingly.

Rosalind's face showed increased confusion with Nathan's rapid questions and statements.

'Na, Na, Nathan,' her words tumbling out. 'I remember, I remember. I can remember things from then, although things are a little hazy. It's the new things I find difficult to remember.'

Nathan reminded her of the stories she'd told him about her experiences on the road, travelling with a group of 'New-Agers', particularly their experiences at 'The Battle of the Beanfield'. That they had been moved on from several sites by the police and finally ending up cornered in a field of beans, resulting in, as she put it, Gestapo-type violence from the police.

'Yesh,' she smiled. 'I v-va-vaguely remember those times. I was very young. It all seems so distant now. In fact everything seems vaguely distant now. But I remember you well,' she stated, changing tack, as if she was suddenly aware of his presence and feelings. 'I have forgotten a lot of things, but I remember our time together. You were my lovely innocent, a person I cared for and felt I could rely on.'

Her slurred speech and mobility were the only apparent things Nathan saw differently in her. These he quickly overlooked, instead adopting a caring approach towards her. A strong, protective feeling of wanting to care for her apparent vulnerability.

Nathan began to pour out his heart. 'I thought about you so much over the years. I was so much in love with you all those years ago and my feelings have not gone away over time. In fact my feelings for you was the only thing that kept me together. I feel that my feelings for you over time have got stronger. I have come back to you.'

A smile came across Rosalind's face. 'That is lovely,' she said. 'When my memory began to came back I thought about you a lot, but, but, I'm married now. Dave has been very good to me. Very kind.'

'Yes, but does he love you?' demanded Nathan.

'N-No. No, please, you must go now,' pleaded a very confused, troubled Rosalind, beginning to get agitated.

Seeing Rosalind's anxiety, Nathan decided that it might be time to withdraw.

'Okay, it might be best if I go now,' he said. 'But can I come and see you again?'

'Yes,' replied Rosalind. 'I would like that. But you must understand that this has been a shock and I find things difficult now.'

'Yes, I understand,' replied Nathan gently. As far as he was concerned he'd made his introduction. He felt he was laying the seeds in her mind about his feelings and any possible future relationship. It was something he felt he could build on over time.

Rising from his chair he stepped across to her. 'I'll see myself out,' he said. 'I'll be back to see you soon. Goodbye for now.' With that he took her hand, kissed it, then turned and walked out of the house. Knowing in his mind that this was not just an obsession, it was now a project, a direction. Rosalind was what he wanted and he felt strongly the need to care for her. That was his future, or so he thought.

CHAPTER 9

REALITY

'If only I could get Rosalind to Castlemorton then it might enable her to recall the past better and our relationship, thereby reviving her feelings for me,' fantasised Nathan to Robbie.

'For Christ's sake Nathan you've got to get real about things,' Robbie lectured him. 'She's been married a long time now, almost as long as me and Angie. With her problems she just ain't going to bugger off, at the drop of a hat, with someone like you who has no money, no job, no place of your own and no immediate future. What you need to do now is get a job, build your future and make it more realistic for her.'

'Get a job!' stormed Nathan rather loudly. 'Fuck off! Just like you I suppose, and you're on the dole!'

'Keep your voice down,' said Robbie quietly, glancing around him.

They were in a pub in the city centre and Nathan's tone of voice had begun to gain glances from the other pub users.

'Well, what fucking chance have I got of getting a job?' said Nathan in a quieter voice.

'Look mate,' said Robbie in a calm tone. 'It's great having you back, but it worries me. If Grivens' scum gets hold of you then God knows what will happen to you. I just don't want to see you injured or even dead. We really need to think where you can go, get away from things, start life again. The way things are it just ain't going to easy for you around here.'

'Yeah, I know,' accepted Nathan. 'But I feel trapped, I still feel there is mileage in a future relationship with Ros. It just needs time and to achieve that I've got to stay around here.'

At that moment a rather chaotically dressed, tall, thin man in his mid-twenties interrupted them. 'Oy ya, Rob,' he said, smiling as he approached their table. 'I ain't sin ya for a long time and I keep getting into trouble with me money.'

'Sit down Georgie,' said Robbie. 'I'll get you a drink. What is it, shandy?'

'Na,' grinned Georgie. 'I'll have a cider.'

'Better be careful of the old applejack,' laughed Robbie. 'We don't want to get you pissed.' Robbie then turned to Nathan. 'Nathan, this is Georgie, he was one of my clients when I was working.' Then turning back to Georgie he said, 'I used to make sure you managed okay in the community didn't I?'

'Yeah, I wish you were back, nobody helps me much now,' declared a rather sombre Georgie.

Robbie rose up, went to the bar and came back with a pint of cider, which he placed in front of Georgie.

'So Robbie used to help you did he?' asked Nathan.

Georgie grinned shyly and nodded.

'Yes, Georgie has a learning disability and he lives in the community, but he needs a lot of support, he can easily get exploited,' Robbie explained to Nathan. Then turning to Georgie he asked, 'How are things in your flat?'

'Kev gave me a fiver to keep more bags of stuff under the bath. I mustn't take the side off the bath, must I? He said he'd give me a kicking if I did.'

'Still up to their old tricks are they? The bastards!' stormed Robbie.

'What's this all about then? Who's Kev anyway?' asked Nathan.

'You may well ask,' said Robbie. 'He's one of Grivens' scum and he lives in the same block as Georgie. We saw him the other day at Castlemorton. They've obviously had a delivery of drugs. They manage to keep it out of sight should the police raid, by hiding it with rather vulnerable people.'

'Can't we do something about this sort of thing?' asked Nathan.

'Well just think about it,' Robbie explained. 'Grivens' scum will just deny things if the cops are called in. What worries me is that it could make things very difficult for Georgie. Either the police could charge Georgie with possession, or if they believe it is one of Grivens' scum and say someone like Kev gets arrested then the other Grivens thugs would rearrange Georgie's features. I don't want to be responsible for whatever happens. Anyway, I've got to be careful, they know I used to work with Georgie, so if any finger gets pointed at me then that worries me, having three kids and a wife, they tend to go for the easy targets. Things are never easy. Anyway I'm glad I'm out of it now. You know, I might be talking like some old git, but life nowadays seems centred around useless bastards. You open magazines, newspapers and even television; it all seems centred on nothing other than useless bastards who gain fame for the sake of it just through publicity. You ask what do they do, what have they done for society? Even politicians want to get in on the act. It's a reward for doing fuck-all culture. In this life if you try to do something useful, what do you get? Crap wages and no recognition!'

Nathan and Georgie began to stare at him, Georgie with his mouth open, looking rather startled.

Robbie, realising he'd got rather carried away, stopped and paused for a few seconds. 'Anyway,' he continued, 'I've had my rant and I'll shut up now.'

'Yeah,' said Nathan, starting to look thoughtful. 'The way I see things is that politics hasn't helped. New Labour, which are just a middle-class bunch, were so in love with Thatcherism that they continued with it, and now the Tories are repeating, but worse. It's all about making big money now. The little man or woman; the working-class, don't count anymore. That's why we're in the shit we're in I can't see any future for myself, that's why I just want a little bit of happiness with Rosalind.'

CHAPTER 10

FINANCIAL SECURITY

The next morning Nathan visited the solicitors that held details of his father's estate. After his father had died, the house was sold and because it had been in joint ownership with his former wife, Nathan's mother, she had received her half of the sale. However, as directed in his father's will, Nathan was to have his half, which was to be shared with his brother in Canada, plus whatever meagre savings he'd had.

The solicitor informed him that this would be transferred to him shortly. It was a nice amount of £45,000, which gave Nathan financial security and some confidence for his future. His chances of getting a job were remote, what with his record and lack of work skills and experience, plus the fact there were several million unemployed. However, he now felt that he had something, some capital, which would enable him to start afresh in another part of the country where no one knew him. But to complete this dream of a new life he needed one person to make it ideal for him, and that person was Rosalind.

Nathan hadn't seen her for two days and he wondered whether things had sunk in regarding his return and any possible feelings for him. He felt he'd certainly made his feelings very clear to her and hoped that memories of their time together would flood back. He decided that he would visit her tomorrow and push his case further; after all, he felt she'd initially been very welcoming of him.

CHAPTER 11

TOGETHER AGAIN

Assuming that her husband was on the same duty as his first visit, Nathan set off to the Westside. As anticipated, Rosalind was again on her own. She opened the door and this time there was complete recognition of Nathan and her face beamed brightly with a wide smile.

'Nathan, it's so nice to see you again. Come in,' said Rosalind, waving him inside.

They sat, drank coffee, and talked about old times, with Nathan having to recall many of their past exploits for Rosalind. They laughed together, sometimes loudly and at times throwing their arms around one another in joy as past pleasant events and experiences were recalled. The warmth of their togetherness made the morning seem completely timeless. The more they recalled happier, joyful times and events, the more physically affectionate they became, and in the end they began to kiss passionately, with their arms tightly locked around one another.

'This is what I've been waiting for, all those years locked away from you,' whispered Nathan, as they paused in their passionate embrace. 'This is what I want and I must have you. We must get away together, you and I, just like we were years ago.'

'Yes, I understand Nathan,' replied a slightly agitated Rosalind. 'I, I love you dearly too, but those times were so far away, we've all changed now. I'm very fond of Dave; he has been very good to me. I'm not sure how I would have managed without him. So please understand, life is very different for me now and as much as I love you, it would be wrong to change things. It is so difficult for me to remember those times now. That period of my life is very cloudy.'

'Yes,' interrupted Nathan. 'If I could take you back to the places we spent good times together, then I'm sure your feelings for our life together will come back.'

'Please, please, you must understand,' responded Rosalind. 'Dave has been very good to me. He helped me off drugs. I owe it to him to keep clean.'

'Well you know you'd be clean with me,' stated Nathan. 'I had no truck with hard drugs, although it would have been very easy for me to have gone that way.'

'I know,' replied Rosalind. 'But it's not just that, Dave helped me so much; I owe him so much.'

'Yes, but do you love him?' questioned Nathan.

'Love comes in many shapes and forms,' replied Rosalind.

'But not in the passionate, romantic sense with Dave?' asked Nathan.

Rosalind did not reply.

'Ros, I want you so much. I need you so much,'

continued Nathan earnestly.

'I don't know Nathan, I'm feeling very confused now. I just don't know what to think anymore. Things are not easy for me now, I get panicky about new ideas, so what you're saying to me makes me feel very unsettled.' Rosalind began to look as if she was struggling with the emotional consequences of the renewed relationship.

'I think I understand,' replied Nathan. 'But please think about us being together. Perhaps if I can take you someplace where we spent time together then I'm sure the thoughts and feelings you had all those years ago will fully return. Please, please think about it. I'll come back and see you again.'

Not waiting for a reply, Nathan bent his head down and kissed Rosalind on the cheek. 'I'll see you again soon. Goodbye my lovely.'

'Goodbye,' replied a rather sad and confused Rosalind.

Nathan felt he had pushed things as far as he could; he now needed to go away and think of an action plan and return to implement it. Leaving the house, he felt reasonably happy with how things were going.

However unknown to him, Rosalind's raised emotions caused her to fall to the floor, having an epileptic fit.

CHAPTER 12

IN PURSUIT

Leaving Rosalind's, Nathan slowly walked down the street. Walking in the direction of the City Centre he suddenly became aware of a car pulling up by his side. The doors on the car on the driver's passenger side and the back passenger door swung open.

Nathan looked around and there was Lump and Kev, advancing towards him. The driver stayed in the car with the engine running.

'Handcock, we want you,' said a grinning Kev as he advanced towards Nathan.

Nathan immediately kicked him in the groin and Kev fell over in pain, grasping at his testicles. Lump, who was advancing fairly quickly behind Kev, immediately fell over him, resulting in the two of them rolling around on the pavement.

Nathan, not wanting to tangle with the three of Corbett's thugs, particularly as two of them would be rather aggressively angry by now, decided to make a run for it.

Just down the road on the other side of the street a bus had just stopped at a bus stop to pick up a passenger. Nathan made an instant decision and ran across the busy A44, just avoiding a car. The car was followed by a line of traffic, which held back the pursuit of Corbett's thugs.

Reaching the bus, Nathan slapped a £10 note onto the cash section of the driver's door. 'Don't worry about the change yet mate,' he said to the driver. 'I'll pick it up when we get there, but can you get a move on? You see those three blokes over there trying to cross the road? One of them is the husband of a woman I've been seeing, so you'll understand my urgency.'

'Been a naughty boy then?' laughed the driver, closing the door and moving the bus forward.

'By the way, where are we going?' asked Nathan, sitting down behind the driver.

The driver laughed again. 'Why, do you want to go all the way? Because we're going to Bromyard.'

'Bromyard!' exclaimed Nathan.

'Yeah, Bromyard, ya know, in Herefordshire,' chuckled the driver.

'Okay, never mind,' snapped back Nathan. 'I'll make up my mind where to get off as we go along.'

Seeing the bus move off, Lump and the others quickly scrambled back into their car. Nathan gave them a mock smile and raised his hand cynically in a royal-type wave as the bus passed them by.

The bus passed out of the city boundary into the Worcestershire countryside. Nathan turned to look out of the back window of the bus. 'Shit!' he muttered to himself as he saw Lump and co. following in their car. *Surely they won't follow too far*, Nathan thought to himself.

They passed through the village of Broadwas and

still the car followed, and Nathan began to get rather agitated.

The view began to change dramatically as they passed the stunning scenery of Ankerdine Hill, with the attractive village of Knightwick nestling below the hillside as the beautiful River Teme gushed by. This took Nathan back to his childhood memories when he visited the area with his parents for picnics and walks.

From there they passed into Herefordshire. Passing Whitbourne, Nathan could still see the others in pursuit. The bus began to climb through the attractive, but mysterious, fern-strewn countryside landscape of Bringsty Common. Tall thickets of bracken covered the Common as far as one could see.

Glancing behind, Nathan could see that they were still being followed. Seeing the landscape, it struck him that this might be the ideal territory to give them the slip, particularly as he thought they were unlikely to expect him to get off in such an area.

'Okay driver,' he shouted. 'I'm getting off here.'

Stopping at the nearest convenient stopping place, the driver opened the door and Nathan began to dash down the steps.

The bus had stopped by a roadside sign which read: 'Live and Let Live', directing one to a pub on the common. Nathan briefly registered the name as an appropriate, but hopefully optimistic sign to his predicament.

'Hey what about your change?' shouted the driver.

'Keep it,' Nathan snapped back over his shoulder.

Jumping from the bus, he ran through a clearing in

the ferns as fast as he could, hoping those in pursuit hadn't seen him leave the bus.

Reaching an outcrop of tall ferns, he dived in, but soon discovered that the ferns were unlikely to hide him stood up. He remembered playing and hiding in the ferns as a young person whenever he and his family visited. He'd so easily forgotten that what he'd done as a smaller individual, he could no longer do now. His only option was to crawl through the ferns, which proved very painful to his hands and knees.

The pursuers almost missed Nathan's exit from the bus, but unfortunately for him one of them caught a glimpse of his back as he disappeared into the ferns. Carl, the driver, slammed on the brakes, to which Lump and Kev threw open the cars doors and dashed out. Carl parked the car just off the road on the edge of the Common and then followed the other two.

Nathan was aware of them and lay down flat amongst the ferns.

Kev picked up a stick and began slashing at the ferns haphazardly. The other two spread out, kicking and lashing at the ferns in their search.

Nathan realised that he would eventually be found just lying in the ferns, so he decided to make a run for it.

There was a shout from the other three as Nathan emerged out of the bracken and he began to run wildly, in no set direction, further into the Common. However, as he passed a thicket of young oak trees he felt a sickening blow to the back of his head. Carl, the driver, stood over him with a hefty piece of wood in his hand that he'd just clubbed Nathan with. Nathan sank into unconsciousness.

CHAPTER 13

CAPTURE

When Nathan came round he found that the back of his head ached like hell. In his state of semi-consciousness he went to raise his hand to feel the back of his head but soon discovered he was unable to; he was sat in an old ricketty, wooden carver-type dining chair with his arms taped to the chair arms. His mouth was also taped.

As his sight began to focus he could see Lump standing leering at him. Sat on a nearby table swinging his legs was Kev. They appeared to be in a type of warehouse. Recognising a familiar smell, Nathan looked around towards the top of the warehouse where he could see cannabis plants in full growth under heat lamps.

The door opened and in walked the large, imposing figure of Dwayne Grivens. His entrance immediately brought an atmosphere of fear to the room. Kev immediately jumped down from the table and stood upright. Lump also appeared to physically straighten his standing posture.

'Well, well, you've finally got the bastard,' snarled Grivens, glaring down at Nathan. He bent down and tore the tape away from Nathan's mouth. Then bending further down, he stared, almost nose to nose, into Nathan's face. 'I'm going to enjoy knocking the fucking shit out of you. You're goin' to have to pay for what you did to my brother. And when I've beaten the shit out of you I'm then going to cut you up and feed you to my pigs. Oink, oink, snork, snork,' he shouted, breathing heavily into Nathan's face, turning his face and laughing loudly at the others. The others responded by returning the laughter as if it was an order.

Nathan turned his head to one side, screwing up his face due to the strong smell of Asian food and alcohol on Grivens' breath.

'God you stink,' spluttered Nathan.

Grivens stood up straight with a surprised look on his face. He looked around at the others, watching their expressions and then he began to laugh out loud. The others, as if given permission, began to laugh as well.

Grivens then took off his coat, handed it to one of the group, rolled up the sleeves of his shirt and then stepped back to take a swing at Nathan.

Nathan could see the club hammer in Grivens' belt and he felt that if he started using that then his end was near. He pulled at the tape on his arms, they felt secure, but the arms of the chair felt loose. In fact as he moved his body within the chair he could feel the chair move as if the joints of the chair were loose. The whole chair seemed quite unstable.

As Grivens swung his right fist at Nathan, he attempted to avoid the punch by ducking his head and moving his whole body vigorously to his left, which resulted in Grivens' fist glancing past Nathan's right cheek.

With his abrupt movement in the chair, it toppled over, and as it went over Nathan instinctively raised up his right foot in a kicking motion, catching Grivens solidly in the crotch, whereby he fell to his knees with a yelp of pain. The chair crashed to the floor, resulting in it falling apart.

Nathan's arms were still taped tightly to the chair arms, but with a sharp pull they came away from the rest of the chair.

On seeing Grivens slump to his knees, Lump and Kev stood momentarily frozen to the spot. Those few seconds gave Nathan just enough time to pull himself to his feet.

On seeing this, Lump and Kev moved forwards to restrain Nathan, but with two wooden chair arms attached to him they quickly proved to be more help than a hindrance and Nathan was able to use them as cudgels, at first warding off many of the punches from the two and then as a means to club both of them to the ground.

With Lump and Kev crouching on the ground, bleeding profusely from wounds on their heads, and Corbett still groaning and holding his crotch, they made a rather pathetic sight.

On his quick exit to the door, Nathan turned and kicked Grivens squarely in the centre of his back with such force that it sent him crashing downwards onto the ground, smashing his face.

'Fat bastard,' he yelled at Grivens.

Nathan opened the door, ran through the rest of the warehouse, and rushed out onto a courtyard, down an alleyway and onto the street. Several passers-by looked on in astonishment as Nathan tore at the tapes with his teeth, managing to tear them free and pull the chair arms off.

As Nathan ran down the street, as fast as he could go to get away, it began to dawn on him that, although he'd had some luck up until now, he'd just about signed his own death warrant with his last actions; it was likely to make Grivens quite mad in his intent towards Nathan. People like Grivens were just not going to fail with him again. It became very clear to Nathan that he now needed to move fast to further his desired future direction.

CHAPTER 14

REALISATION

'What the bloody hell have you been up to?' exclaimed Jack Armstrong, staring at the bruises and cuts to Nathan's face.

Nathan grinned, as best he could, however rather sheepishly. 'I encountered the rather dubious characters of the City,' he replied.

'Like who?' questioned a puzzled-looking Jack.

'Dwayne Grivens for a start,' replied Nathan. 'He, as you may recall, has a vendetta going back over twenty years, he wants to settle with me.'

'Scum like that need to be jumped on,' stormed Jack. 'Going back thirty to forty years, scum like that would have been just street corner thugs, but now they're bleeding business men; if you can call them that. Drug businessmen, pushing drugs to the despondent, the feckless and the stupid. Corrupting the very structure of society, making those addicted, prisoners of their own doom. Years ago there were proud family structures, their kids had apprenticeships; prospects of a craft they could take with them all their life; something to take pride in. But what have they got now? Just shit politicians of all parties, with no real life experiences, filling their own bleeding pockets, destroying communities with their stupid, poncey ideas. Our identity is being destroyed now.'

Nathan began to look impatient, but Jack continued regardlessly.

'We need a strict Socialist regime, not this wet Tory, New Labour farcical bunch. We need to get back to basics; get some moral backbone back into society. You know, my teenage nephew recently told me he no longer felt safe living in a small rural town. This state of affairs is shocking for the future of our young, I feel really sorry for the young today. Things are changing so quickly, too quickly for the general good. I'd bet you've seen some changes since you came out. Things were starting to change quite rapidly when you went into prison, but technology is moving so fast that the future looks too bleak for the general good. When I left school in the 50s it was expected that you got a job, be an apprentice or something. What we've got now is the acceptance that many will never work, with exposure to the scum that destroys society and shit politicians. Society seems to be controlled now by greedy bankers and tax-dodging billionaires.

'The beauty is being tainted further in other directions. You know, the idiots who take the drugs that the scum push out are bad enough, adding to the general destruction of society. But the bastards who push them are the architects of destruction; the demons, who really taint the beauty.'

'But surely things must have changed for the better,' questioned Nathan.

'CHANGE?' roared Jack. 'Change? Change, it never happens, as long as you've got greedy bastards in control, where greed is their god. All we get from politicians now is the political bullshit of austerity and deficit fetishism. The poor have to suffer for the good of the bleedin' wealthy. The rich now have a greater share of the wealth. Wealth never trickles down down, it only trickles up, leaving the scum to tear at the flesh and gnaw at the bones of the poor. All they give us back is their talk of aspirations, that people should have aspirations. But aspirations for what? Not for care, or community, or a decent job that isn't zero hours, but for greed. Aspirational greed, it just demeans the human species. Aspiration, they might as well say we've fucked up the country, but we're all right, so just fuck off and sort yourselves out.'

'Yeah, yeah,' grunted Nathan, grimacing. 'I'm sure it was good years ago, more structured and all that, but this is how it is now. Scum from the top to the bottom rule the roost. I don't know what the answer is, but I just know I've got to get away, because if I stay here any longer then I'm dead meat.'

'As bad as that?' questioned Jack, with a worried but caring expression on his face.

'You bet. I've just got to get away,' replied a rather despondent Nathan.

'Well, I'll help as much as I can,' said Jack. 'I've got a few quid I could loan you.'

'Thanks Jack,' said Nathan. 'I appreciate that, but Dad left me some money so that will keep me going for a bit. But if I can think of anything you can do then I'll let you know. I need to make a few phone calls, then I want to get a few hours' kip; I've got a lousy headache. If things work out okay I might be on my way tomorrow.'

'Anyway, talking about your dad,' said Jack. 'I know younger people nowadays don't seem to bother much about this sort of thing, but my generation believed in showing some respect for the dead. I mean, you never had chance to attend his funeral so do you think you should pay a last visit to his grave before you go away?'

'Yeah,' replied Nathan. 'I really should try, I think I owe him that at least.'

'I really believe you should,' continued Jack. 'You know I think a lot of his problems started years ago. Do you remember that time, you must have been about fifteen, or something, when me and your dad went up to London to support the printers outside Fortress Wapping?'

Nathan nodded. He then stopped to think for a few moments, and then looked up. 'Yeah. What really happened then?'

'Well,' Jack started. 'Fortress Wapping was a horrible place, a very restrictive area, with the frontage covered in razor sharp barbed wire for about a hundred yards right up to the front of the building. It was in the early hours of the morning, there was a very large crowd, several hundred yards deep supporting the pickets. Suddenly the police went berserk and charged at the crowd on horseback, swinging large truncheons. Well, as you can imagine, there was absolute panic amongst the crowd and people where running like mad to escape from the area. A poor woman fell nearby and you could hear the crunch as she broke her shoulder. I stopped with the fellow she was with to help her up and to safety and that's when I lost track of your dad. He was later found unconscious by some of our group and they carried him back to the bus where he regained consciousness. I bet you remember that nasty bruising to his neck and shoulder that he had?'

'Yes, I do,' replied a rather stern Nathan.

'You know he never really got over that,' replied Jack. 'Whatever happened there, then the loss of his job later, really led him into depression. Horrible times, horrible times.' Jack stood in thought for a few moments. 'You know,' he continued, 'in those days we used to refer to the coppers as Thatcher's Stormtroopers, but they seem to be getting a bit of a taste of their own medicine now with the way that they are being treated. I hear they are having their numbers cut and their pensions reduced. What comes around goes around. The bastards in control don't give a shit about anyone but themselves. Anyway, I don't suppose you want to hear me blathering on. I'd better sort you out.'

'No, it was enlightening, useful. Thanks Jack, I'll try and make it to Dad's grave,' replied a rather thoughtful Nathan.

'Well good. But anyway I'll be sorry to see you go,' stated a rather saddened Jack. 'Good luck lad. Hey, but what about your mate Robbie? Don't you want to say goodbye?'

'Yeah, I really should,' said Nathan. 'Although I've

got to be careful going out.'

'I'll tell you what, I'll drop you off there, but order a taxi back,' said Jack. 'Don't give Grivens' yobs the opportunity to get you by you using public transport back.'

CHAPTER 15

LAST GOODBYES

There was no obvious sign of Grivens or his thugs when Jack drove him to Robbie's. Nathan assumed that they were licking their wounds after their confrontation earlier. Either that, or they were planning something more unpleasant for him the next day. However, he was aware that what had happened that day was very likely to make matters a lot worse for him. Grivens would undoubtedly be hopping mad. There was now no doubt in Nathan's mind that he would just have to make a break and get away the next day.

Robbie and Angie were pleased to see him. However, they expressed concerns about his appearance.

'What the hell happened to you?' asked Robbie.

'Oh, I had a little confrontation with Grivens and his colleagues,' Nathan responded wryly.

'Good grief! This ain't right Nathan,' said a concerned Robbie. 'You're just going to have to sort out your future from now on. Anyway, changing the subject, it's great to see you mate, come on in, we'll have a chat. The kids seem fairly okay at the moment, so sit down and I'll get you a beer.'

It was early evening and the children were watching television, with a little supper, before going to bed.

'Thanks,' said Nathan, walking into the living room and sitting down. 'You can probably guess but after today I feel I need a beer or two. Hey, I'll tell you what, this is a bit cheeky, but could I have a sandwich as well? I haven't eaten much today and I'm starving.'

'Sure, no problem,' said Angie. 'Cheese okay? It'd better be, it's all we've got.'

'Yes great,' replied Nathan. 'I could eat a horse.'

Robbie got a couple of cans of lager and he and Nathan sat down. Angie returned with the sandwich and sat down as well.

'Our only luxury now, this cheap lager,' said Robbie to Nathan.

'What, no lager for me?' mocked Angie.

'Sorry did you want one?' said an apologetic Robbie. 'You don't usually.'

'Na,' she laughed. 'I was only winding you up.'

Nathan took a bite out of his sandwich and when he'd chewed up and swallowed his mouthful, he looked up earnestly at the other two.

'Look you two,' he said. 'You've been brilliant to me, standing by me. Not many people would, especially after all these years. But basically what I've come for today is to say goodbye. Hopefully not, but it's possible I may never see you again.'

'You what!' Robbie and Angie spluttered out in

harmony. They looking at one another, aware of their co-ordinated response and chuckled, but then immediately changed to more serious expressions.

'Yeah,' continued Nathan. 'Things have got really difficult for me. Grivens nearly beat the shit out of me today, but I got lucky and managed to get away with just a few cuts and bruises, as you can see.'

'Well, unfortunately, I must say I'm not surprised,' stated Robbie. 'I felt you were mad to return to this area. You will recall I did warn you. It worried me that you came back, not that I don't want to see you, but I knew Grivens wouldn't let things lie. That's the way he operates. It's his way or nothing.'

Angie nodded her agreement.

'Look Nathan,' she said. 'I can understand how you feel about Ros, but don't you think you're pushing your feelings onto her? After all, she's been married a long time and as you must have found out now, she's got a lot of problems. Not that you couldn't be of help to her, I'm sure you could and would, but just think of it, looking after Ros with Grivens breathing down your neck all the time.'

'Yes, ready to do you serious damage,' interrupted Robbie in agreement.

'Yeah, I know,' said Nathan, taking a swig from his lager. 'But this all matters to me; seeing Ros, being with her. It's important to me, I just can't get her out of my head. You've got to realise that.'

'We know, Nathan,' said Robbie. 'I can guess how I'd feel without Ange, it would devastate me. But your case is different. Get yourself away. Find yourself a good hideout somewhere and hopefully after time things might calm down. You never know, if Ros feels she wants to join up with you in the future then perhaps we could arrange things this end with her.'

'Yeah, well I'm going to see her tomorrow,' stated Nathan. 'It's going to be a do or die mission. If she insists on staying, then I can't force her; I suppose I'll have to accept it. But you can take it from me that I'm going to have a damn good try tomorrow to persuade her to come away with me. After all, as far as I'm concerned, life would just not be right without her. That's all I've thought about for over twenty years.'

After a few more lagers, a taxi was ordered and Nathan said his farewells. He hugged them both and a few tears were shed.

'Well goodbye mate,' said Robbie, as the taxi arrived. 'Look after yourself and let us know how you're getting on. Now that you're going, I feel better in my mind that you'll be safer away from here.'

Nathan left the house with a lump in his throat, hoping that he would be able to see them in the future if his situation ever became less dangerous.

Watching the taxi drive away with Nathan inside, Angie turned to Robbie and said, 'You know, I think he's obsessed.'

'I'm inclined to agree with you,' said Robbie.

CHAPTER 16

THE LAST THROW OF
THE DICE

The next morning Nathan got up early. He walked into the kitchen where Jack was eating his breakfast.

'Gosh, you're up early,' said a surprised Jack. 'What's you got lined up, something special?'

'Yeah,' replied Nathan. 'I've really got to sort things out today.'

'Wise man,' said Jack, getting up from the table. 'I'm goin' to stroll into town to get a paper and a few other things before the crowds start. I'll see you later.'

'Yeah,' replied Nathan, knowing full well that it was most unlikely that they would see one another again, with what he had in mind. 'Anyway, thanks for everything Jack.'

Jack paused by the kitchen door on his way out of the room, frowning at Nathan's last statement. He looked back at Nathan but after a short pause he continued on his journey.

From his phone call the previous day Nathan knew that Rosalind would be on her own; her husband Dave was on early duty. Taking Jack at his word of offering help, he decided to take his car. Although he hadn't driven since before he was in prison, however, he felt he needed to take a chance by driving.

Before he left Nathan placed a note where Jack would see it, explaining he was taking the car, thanking him for his help and promising to leave it somewhere safe where he could pick it up afterwards.

Knowing where Jack kept his car keys, Nathan took them and quietly left the house. Jack's car was conveniently parked outside on the street.

Nathan cautiously drove away. However, unseen by him, a hooded youth stepped out from behind a wall and made a call on his mobile.

Arriving at at Rosalind's, Nathan reversed onto the front drive. He rang the doorbell and after a lengthy interval Rosalind answered the door. She was still in her night-clothes; a short nightie with a dressing gown, open at the front and hanging loosely from her shoulders. She looked as if she had just got out of bed.

'Hoy,' said Nathan, greeting her with a smile.

Rosalind returned a sleepy smile without saying anything. She turned and began walking back up the hallway.

Closing the door behind him, Nathan followed her up the hallway. Halfway up he impatiently put his hands on her hips, pulling her towards him and around so that she faced him.

'Ros, things are getting very difficult for me living around here,' he said, his face so close to hers that

that their noses nearly touched. 'I really have to get away and I want you to come with me.'

'Oh. Oh no, I don't know,' she replied, looking very confused. 'Dave has been very good to me. I just couldn't leave him.'

'Please, please Ros. I want you so much, I thought of nothing else all those years I was in prison. Life would not be right for me now if I didn't have you. I must have you,' he demanded passionately.

'Oh, Nathan, I just don't know.'

At this, Nathan decided he needed to be even more positive. He pulled her to him and began kissing her passionately. Rosalind made no attempt to break away and returned the passion.

Kissing her, Nathan's left arm was around her waist and his right hand was on her left hip. As they kissed, he slid his right hand further down her hip, past her night-dress, reaching bare leg. Raising his hand up the inside of her leg, under her night-dress, he reached between her legs. Half caressing her pubic hairs, he slid his middle finger inside her vagina. There was no resistance from Rosalind. He started slowly and then began moving his finger more rapidly as her vagina moistened. After a little while, Rosalind gave a little half-cry moan and shuddered.

Taking his finger away, Nathan looked Rosalind directly in her eyes. 'Ros, I want you so much, I'm desperate for you,' he pleaded. 'Let's go upstairs,' he proposed, whispering in her ear.

Rosalind pulled back at that, as if the full realisation of the last few minutes had suddenly dawned on her.

'No, oh no. I just can't let this happen,' she stated in an upset, but defiant tone. 'Dave has been so good to me, I owe him so much. Nathan, I love you dearly, but I just cannot allow this to continue. Please, don't you see?'

Nathan stepped back, realising that in one sense he had perhaps overstepped the mark. He took a deep breath, which helped him cool down a little. After a few seconds of inner thought he came to the conclusion that he was easy about Rosalind's reticence; he certainly didn't want it to be a 'wham, bang, thank you ma'am' experience for her. After all, he thought, he'd waited twenty-three years, so a few more days didn't make much difference.

His years in prison thinking about Rosalind had kept his body and mind together. But thinking and planning about her had led to an obsession in his mind. He was totally single-minded about it and like many obsessions it was only a step away from madness. He had run things over in his mind over and over again. So far, things were going reasonably to plan. The situation regarding Rosalind's acquired brain injury was perhaps unexpected, but it made not the slightest difference to his obsessional feelings, perhaps bringing out his feelings of wanting to care for her. In a way, he subconsciously felt that his caring response could negate any possible resistance from her and contribute to making her dependant upon him.

'Okay, Ros, I understand, it is very difficult for both of us. But, just for my sake at least, let me take you out to see something. I promise that if what I show you doesn't help in any decision-making of yours, then I will bring you back. But please, I beg you, do this for me. Because I've really got to leave this area. I may never see you again and the very thought of that tears me apart. So please, please help me,' Nathan pleaded.

'Where will we go?' asked Rosalind.

'A place that you know well. Just a few miles up the road,' replied Nathan.

Nathan had it set in his mind that if he could get Rosalind to see Castlemorton again, even after all those years, and she could dance on the Common again, although perhaps not as well as previously, then all the thoughts and feelings of their time together would flood back. It was his last desperate throw of the dice. If he could just get her away from this house, which appeared to be her security, her crutch, her comfort zone, then she might just reject what he saw as her present comfortable, rut-like existence.

'Well, okay. This is very difficult for me. I just can't give up everything, but I will allow you this request, because the very thought of not seeing you again I find very upsetting.'

'And that's the way I would feel if I never saw you again,' said Nathan. 'It would absolutely devastate me.'

'Where would you go?' asked Rosalind.

'I don't know,' replied Nathan. 'The Forest of Dean, Wye Valley areas might be a good start. I could lose myself there for a bit. But I may need to go further afield, such as the Shropshire Hills or even as far as Scotland.'

'Okay, I'll go with you on this short trip, but you must bring me back. Now I need to get dressed. Just wait while I put on some clothes.'

She turned and walked up the hallway to the stairs. Nathan watched as she very ponderously and very slowly climbed the stairs.

After what seemed a long time, but could only have been about ten minutes at the most, Rosalind appeared at the top of the stairs, fully dressed, and began walking downstairs, again very ponderously.

'Okay, let's go,' said Nathan, opening the front door.

He helped Rosalind into the car and drove out of the drive in the direction of Castlemorton.

What he didn't see was a car with four people inside, which had been parked up the street, follow them as they moved away.

CHAPTER 17

THE MESSAGE

As Nathan and Rosalind left the house and drove away, they were also being watched from a different direction. Molly, the young neighbour, stood at her window with her baby in her arms. Seeing Rosalind leave with Nathan seemed to jolt her into action. She turned from the window and walked briskly across the room .the telephone. Putting the baby down safely, she dialled a number she had been given by Dave Barnes.

'Dave, is that you?' asked Molly, as a voice came on the line. 'It's Molly,' she said.

'Oh, okay. Is this an emergency? You know I've told you only to use this number if it is, otherwise I could get into trouble,' replied Dave.

'Well, I'm not sure. It could be,' answered Molly. 'Perhaps I should have told you before. But what with the baby and everything. Well anyway, it's just that a fellow, I've never seen before, called to see Ros a few days ago. He called again yesterday and as he left the house there were some men outside waiting for him. There was a bit of a punch-up and the fellow ran off. Well the situation became even stranger today when the fellow called again and after about half an hour or so he came out with Ros. They got into his car and drove away. But what is perhaps most worrying, is that some of the fellows who had been waiting outside yesterday, were hanging around outside today and on occasions returning to a car parked up the street. When Ros and the fellow drove away they followed them.'

'Bloody hell!' stormed Dave. 'What the bloody hell's going on?'

'I'm sorry I didn't tell you anything before but it didn't seem to be anything until yesterday and then today things seem to have got stranger. I'm so sorry,' whimpered Molly.

'Okay, sorry about my outburst. Thanks for telling me, Molly,' said a worried Dave. 'Ros apparently had a small fit yesterday; she hasn't had one for years so she's lucky she didn't choke. So what's going on may have something to do with it. I may have to arrange to take her to see the doctor; it looks like she may have to go back on medication. Although she seemed okay last night and when I left this morning. However, I asked my mother to drop in today to keep an eye on her, but obviously she hasn't arrived yet. Did you get a description of the car, and what did the fellow look like who went off with Ros?'

'It was a green car, dark green, a Rover I think, an old car,' answered Molly.

'What about the other car?' Dave asked.

'I don't know what it was, but it was silver grey, a flashy, expensive-looking car. Whoever owned it must be loaded. Anyway they both went in the direction of town,' replied Molly.

'Did you get the car registrations — the car numbers?' asked Dave.

'Yes,' replied Molly and gave them to him.

'Thanks, that's great,' said Dave. 'Tell me, what did the fellow look like who went with Ros?'

Molly gave a description of Nathan.

'Oh shit,' retorted Dave. Then realising what he'd just said, he apologised. 'Sorry, but that description sounds very much like someone I may know. Anyway thanks for that Molly, and particularly thanks for the car numbers, they could be very useful. I will now need to speak to my Sergeant to see what we can do. Goodbye and thanks again.'

On leaving the phone call, Dave immediately sought out the Sergeant and explained what he'd just been told.

'Yeah, it does sound a bit fishy,' said Sergeant Boules. 'I can understand why you seem worried. I think in the first instance we'd better get those numbers checked out, then decide where we go from here.'

A little later the news came back that the Rover belonged to Jack Armstrong and the other car to Dwayne Grivens.

'This don't make any sense at all,' said Sergeant Boules. 'I know Jack Armstrong; he's a decent bloke. So who's driving his car, because the description wasn't him, and why is Grivens following it?'

'Well actually, the description of the fellow sounded very much like Nathan Hancock. I understand he's been staying with Jack,' stated Dave.

'I don't like the sound of this,' said Sergeant Boules. 'We'd best put a call out to patrols, etc. We may need to standby for likely trouble. Dave, you'd better stay free for the time being. With your wife involved we may need you. We'd better get someone to check Jack Armstrong to make sure he's okay. I know Jack; he used to be my Councillor. A decent bloke, I wouldn't like to see anything happen to him.'

CHAPTER 18

OPERATIONAL ACTION

'A CID car coming back from Upton-upon-Severn has seen them. They recognised Grivens' flash car,' said Sergeant Boules to Dave Barnes. 'Grivens turned onto the A4104 and seemed to be heading for Malvern. I've told them to follow at a discreet distance, with direct instructions not to be seen if possible. Luckily it's an unmarked car, so they will be in a better position to estimate what's going on, without being obviously on show. We'd better alert our people at Malvern.'

'What about Jack Armstrong?' asked Dave.

'What was the answer, Wilkins?' Sergeant Boules asked WPC Wilkins.

'He seemed okay,' she replied. 'He answered the phone straight away. Apparently he'd just come back from walking into town and found his car missing. In the house was a note from Hancock stating he'd borrowed it. Jack seemed okay about it, but he was a bit disappointed that Hancock hadn't asked him.'

'Look,' said Sergeant Boules, turning back to Dave. 'I don't like the smell of this at all. I remember Hancock's case and he and Grivens are unlikely to be kissing and making up. I'd better inform the top brass about it, also inform CID and the drug people. I know they've been watching Grivens, so this may be their chance of some action. Let's face it he's been very clever up to now. Look, your wife may need you, so grab a partner and a driver, and head in that direction. We'll direct you further, the more information we get.'

Dave took Roger Gwillam, his usual partner, with him and with a driver they set off in the direction of Malvern.

CHAPTER 19

THE RETURN

'I know this place, but what is it? Where are we?' asked Rosalind, gazing out across Castlemorton Common.

'This is where it all kicked off for both of us,' replied Nathan. 'This is the place we last spent real time together. You and I, back in '92.'

Nathan drove further onto the Common, stopped the car, got out and walked around to help Rosalind out. He held her hand as they walked uneasily across the uneven ground of the Common.

'Remember the rave; the festival we all had here? We had real good times together. Remember Somerset? We were together some time down there, it was much more peaceful then, just you and I,' said Nathan, trying to get Rosalind back on track to the better times when they were young.

'Yes, I think I remember it all. This place looks so familiar, yet so different,' replied Rosalind.

Nathan smiled. 'Yes, it was so different then, very dangerous and noisy. Now it's completely different; peaceful and beautiful.'

'It is very beautiful, especially with the hills in the

background. Although a little eerie,' said Rosalind, smiling as she gazed around.

'Eerie?' chuckled Nathan. 'Yes, I think you're right. It's one of those places where eerie and beautiful go together, without being a contradiction.'

'Were we mad to do what we did then?' asked Rosalind.

'Yes, I think we must have been a little,' replied a more serious Nathan, breathing in the air deeply. 'We believed in freedom then, but we also wanted a green, pollution-free planet and then we all come here and temporarily destroy this beautiful, but haunting place.'

Nathan took her hand in his and gazed into her face. 'You know,' he said. 'I've probably said this before, but whenever I'm with you and especially touching you, I get a tingling excitement, a sort of sensual electricity. I really love you. Please say you'll come away with me.'

Rosalind smiled.

They walked further onto the Common, talking, laughing, smiling, and occasionally hugging one another, as if there wasn't a care in the world, totally unaware of who was watching them from the top of the road that led unto the Common.

'Oh, Ros, please say you'll come away with me. I want you so,' pleaded Nathan again.

CHAPTER 20

THE WAIT

'What the bleeding hell are they up to?' stormed DS Paul Ravenshill to DC Dawn Peplow as they watched, from a discreet distance, the stationary car containing Grivens and his cronies.

They were parked as far out of sight as possible, on the side of the road, several hundred metres from Grivens' car, which was parked on the perimeter of the Common.

'What on earth's he up to out here in that car?' questioned DC Peplow. 'He only uses that car when he's trying to make a civic impression; trying to get publicity; to make out he's some kind of good guy.'

'Or impress women; his shagging car,' added DS Ravenshill. 'He must have been out somewhere, clubbing, shagging, whatever, and come out in a heck of a hurry, otherwise why use it?'

'Sounds like he was caught with his trousers down,' giggled DC Peplow. 'So something about this journey must be very important to him.'

'You can bet your life on that,' replied DS Ravenshill.

'Perhaps he's become a nature lover and come out

to have a picnic in style,' smirked DC Peplow.

'No chance of that,' retorted DS Ravenshill. 'He's up to something and you can probably bet that it's something unpleasant. It just don't seem right him being out here. Also where the fuck is the other car that Hancock was driving?'

'They must be watching them on the Common,' said DC Peplow. 'We can't see it too well from here.'

DS Ravenshill grunted in half agreement. 'I don't like this one bit, get on to base and see what backup they're getting to us,' he ordered. 'If anything takes off we haven't got a chance, just the two of us.'

DC Peplow radioed in their concerns and the message came back that backup was already on its way from Malvern and another car was on its way from Worcester.

'Hey hang on, what's happening?' DC Peplow stated excitedly, looking up. 'They're moving off in the direction of the Common.'

'Okay, we'd better follow at a discreet distance,' stated DS Ravenshill. 'But let's hope that backup gets here soon.'

CHAPTER 21

FINALE

'Look we can't hang around for here forever watching that bastard prance about with that bint,' stormed an impatient Grivens to the others in the car, his face showing stubble due to his early call. This and the problems he'd had with Nathan the day before had placed him in a pretty foul mood. 'There's no one else about so let's get in, we'll never have a better chance.'

They drove off through the Common and onto the side road leading to where Nathan had parked his car.

* * *

Nathan, deeply involved with his attention to Rosalind, suddenly became aware that a car had driven up nearby. Despair soon overtook his present state of bliss when he noticed Grivens and three of his thugs get out of the car. They were about twenty metres away and under normal circumstances his instinct would have been to run, but having Rosalind with him, whose mobility wasn't one hundred percent, his options suddenly became extremely limited.

Grivens' three thugs ran towards them and quickly surrounded them. Grabbing hold of Nathan, they dragged him forward so that he was on his knees. Grivens arrived a few seconds later, removed his coat and pulled the club hammer from his belt.

'What's going on?' demanded Rosalind, standing defiantly in Grivens' way.

'Oh fuck off!' Grivens screamed at her, violently pushing her aside, where she fell heavily onto the rough ground.

* * *

'We're going to have to do something,' snapped DS Ravenshill, having watched Corbett push Rosalind to the ground, as they cautiously approached the Common from a distance, just about far enough away to see what was going on. 'Let's run the car up to them, we might stop what's going on. Where the fuck is that support?'

'I'll put an urgent call out for support,' stated DC Peplow. 'It looks like we're going to need it.'

After she'd made the call, they looked at one another. DS Ravenshill nodded and then shouted, 'Well okay, hold tight, we're going in.'

* * *

With Rosalind pushed aside, Grivens stepped forward with the club hammer in his hand. 'Bastard, FUCK-ING bastard,' he screamed hysterically, as he swung the hammer full force at Nathan's head.

The intent of the force of the blow from the hammer, as it smashed into Nathan's head, was such, that blood splattered over those holding him. They immediately let go of him in repulsion, but it made no difference because Nathan died instantly from the blow and he fell to the ground, lifeless.

As Rosalind lay on the ground she pushed her head and shoulders up. Seeing what took place, she immediately began to fit from the shock.

* * *

At that moment the police cars from Malvern arrived. Officers piled out of the cars and at the direction of DS Ravenshill and DC Peplow, Grivens and his thugs were quickly overpowered.

One of the officers examining Nathan turned around to the others and shook his head.

'Got you, at long last, you bastard!' shouted a jubilant DS Ravenshill to Grivens. 'You just ain't going to worm your way out of this one.'

Grivens glared at DS Ravenshill. 'Cunt, fucking cunt,' he snarled as they led him away. 'At least I got the bastard.'

DS Ravenshill laughed back. 'And now we've got you at long last.'

The car containing Dave Barnes arrived and he quickly dashed to where Rosalind lay. 'Get an ambulance!' he screamed.

Nathan's body lay on the ground of Castlemorton Common, a solitary figure having been left abandoned by the examining officers. He'd had his time with Rosalind; a little bit of happiness.

He'd had his day and his day had come and gone.

In the distance the sun passed behind dark clouds, plunging the clear outline of the Malvern Hills into gloom, presenting a depressed, perhaps all-knowing picture of the past viewing the future.

Castlemorton – for some life ended here.

Twenty-three years for killing scum. Twenty-three fucking years!

ABOUT THE AUTHOR

A. C. Dyke has had a vast employment and educational experience. His first degree at Worcester College of Higher Education (now Worcester University) was a Combined Studies Degree in Sociology, Rural Settlement and Land-Use and Ecosystems and Man. After a period working for the Probation Service as a Campaign Co-ordinator, he then went on to study at the Lord Scarman Centre for the Study of Public Order, The University of Leicester, where after two years he gained an MA in Criminology.

After leaving Leicester University he became a Social Worker for Adults with Learning Disabilities. A particularly rewarding role, which gave him vast experience of the difficulties for people with Learning Disabilities and Acquired Brain Injuries living in the community.

Previous to gaining his first degree, he worked in the printing industry for many years at a major book printers' and then at Worcester Evening News. During this period he was a Councillor on Worcester City Council for eight years. Due to the troubles in the printing industry, during the late 1980s, he decided to take redundancy from the printing trade to enable him to study for his degree.

He has also written a trilogy of books for children, also avaliable on Amazon.

TAINTED BEAUTY

Printed in Great Britain
by Amazon